The Partners

One man was named Harry Banner. He was the brains. The other, Roy Walls, was the muscle. Together they formed a perfect team to carry out a perfect plan to kidnap a rich man's little boy and make themselves a mint.

Every angle was carefully calculated before they made their move. The snatch went off smooth as silk. The parents were left helpless, the police baffled.

But Harry and Roy had not reckoned on the bright, sickly, pathetic, trusting little boy himself—and what he could do to them. . . .

TAKING GARY FELDMAN

TAKING GARY FELDMAN

Stanley Cohen

A DELL BOOK

To Marilyn and the Kids

TAKING
GARY
FELDMAN

1

The gray-haired man at the wheel of the laundry truck drove in silence. His younger partner, also wearing a white uniform, was restless and kept bringing his hand up to adjust his glasses. "Don't you turn here?" His voice was high-pitched, almost a toot.

"The next one," said the man driving.

"It's this one."

"Either one gets you there. The next one's a better way. I been over it both ways. Couple of times."

The next road was wider and smoother and less built up, but more densely wooded, the summer greenness emanating a lush, woodsy air. Despite the one or two intersections marked by ornate street signs or an occasional wealthy home deep-set in lawn, the road resembled a main drive in a state park.

"I just hope you got everything right."

"Everything's right. How many times. . . . Jesus!"

"We've gone to a lot of trouble if it's not. One hell of a lot."

"It's right, so relax. He's in Pittsburgh and she's in Europe."

A short distance away, in a massive Tudor house, a frail red-haired boy stood quietly, observing the excitement being created by two small furry animals in a glass and chrome tank. They were possibly his closest friends, his Frederick and Madame George, Muridae family, Rodentia order, Mammalia class, Chordata phylum, Animal kingdom. Under his prolonged and attentive gaze the little beasts made a frantic play world of their shelf-sized rectangular estate. One of them took one, two, three, never more than three, turns in the exercise wheel and then bustled out of it, stopping to sit on tiny haunches and survey the surroundings. The other booted a ping-pong ball which caromed the length of the tank. Cedar chips, a fluff of shredded burlap, a fruit juice can with both ends removed, a suspended feeder bottle, an ear of dried corn, and bits of cereal and lettuce cluttered the tank.

The boy stuck his hands into the tank, and the little fur balls ran up and explored his fingers. Lifting one out by the base of its tail and cupping his other hand under it, he brought it up to his face and nuzzled it. He let it climb up his arm onto his shoulders, lifted it off and, holding it in one hand, petted it with the other. Then, lowering it back into the tank, he watched the two of them for a moment, dropped himself to the carpeted floor and began leafing through a large book illustrated with nature photographs.

The laundry truck turned again, this time onto a road built up with elegant homes. The driveway leading up to the imposing house where the boy lived was more than a hundred yards long. The truck was completely out of sight from the road when it pulled under the arched breezeway. While the driver kept the motor running, the other man stepped from the truck. Pausing a moment to look in all directions, he walked up to the door, tried it slowly, opened it and walked inside.

Upstairs, a young brown maid in a black uniform sat on the shag-carpeted floor in one of the bedrooms. She was slumped against the foot of a bed, dozing, her head resting on the bed, her mouth open. Downstairs in the kitchen the cook was standing at the counter, a two-bladed chopper in her fat black hand pounding away at something in a wooden bowl. She crooned along with a small radio. The boy was still on the floor in the library off the large entry foyer. Somewhat fidgety and listless, he was only partly absorbed by the familiar book in front of him.

The man in white walked quietly to the middle of the foyer. Lean but muscular, and in his thirties, he had a squared face, coarse features and a thick, incongruous mustache. He wore heavy horn-rimmed glasses. Standing motionless for a moment and looking around, he exchanged glances with the boy, who ignored him. Picking up the sounds from the kitchen, he nodded and smiled as if they were exactly as expected.

Holding a forefinger to his lips to suggest silence, he walked toward the boy, who again looked at him with large sad eyes as he entered the room. Although surprised that a laundryman or the like would bother to come over to him, the child did not speak but continued to stare up at him curiously. The man kneeled next to the child, still holding his finger to his lips, and then managed something of a smile. Pausing another moment to recheck the sounds of the house, he suddenly clamped his thick arm around the boy's head, covering the mouth with his fingers and gripping the small nose between thumb and forefinger. Rising to his feet and roughly jerking the child with him, he used his other arm to encircle and subdue the thin, wildly flailing legs.

Moving with quick soundless steps, he went back through the open front door. He tightened his arm around the boy's head but loosened his thumb, allowing the child to breathe. Releasing the boy's legs momentarily, he eased the door closed in perfect quiet and again smothered the renewed frenzy of the small legs as he grabbed the boy up and stepped to the open door of the truck. The man at the wheel flipped the right-hand seat forward, allowing him to scramble with the struggling child into the back of the truck. Locking his legs around the boy's legs, he slid to the floor, keeping the mouth covered. "Move out!"

The driver leaned across, pulled the door closed and headed the truck down the driveway. "Any trouble?"

4

"Nobody around. . . . They don't even know he's gone. . . . We didn't even need the truck." Slightly winded, he spoke in short piping gasps.

"It's better with the truck. What if someone had been around?" Looking in all directions as he drove, he suddenly shook his head and smiled as if pleased. "Not bad. Not bad." He said it out loud, but to himself. "Not bad at all. In fact, easy. Jesus." His smile widened to a grin for a moment and then began to fade, and a character-istic look of pained resignation returned to his face. A thickly built man in his middle forties with quiet eyes under wavy gray hair, he had a handlebar mustache and also wore heavy-rimmed glasses.

The man holding the boy pulled a strip of wide adhesive tape off the wall of the truck with his free hand. The strip was more than two feet long with a pad of gauze stuck to its center. Plac-ing the gauze over the squirming child's eyes, he sealed it completely around the small head. Then he reached for a rumpled pile of bed sheets and pulled them over himself and the boy until they were completely covered.

The child was stifled by the man's strong grip and by the closeness and stagnancy of the air under the sheet. Struggling to breath through his nose, which was beginning to tighten up, he yearned to have his mouth free.

The man smelled. The man's body odor was the ugliest thing he could ever remember smelling. The man's breath was worse. Many times worse. He winced each time the man exhaled and wished

5

he could go without breathing. He concentrated on breathing as little as possible, timing his breaths to avoid those of the man. If only his mouth were free.

He wondered where they were taking him. Where? Where possibly? And why? Who were they? What were they doing with him? . . . Obviously, they had kidnapped him. Yes, kidnapped. *He was being kidnapped!* But there was no point in crying. There was no one to respond. Besides, he couldn't cry. His mouth was covered, and his nose was tightening. He only wished he could be out of the path of the man's breathing. He didn't know how much longer he would be able to endure the tides of ugly stench burning through his thickening nostrils.

The truck continued at normal speed, out of the wealthy suburb and across the city, staying clear of heavy downtown traffic. The man holding the boy relaxed his rigid grip on the boy but did not release him. Sensing the loosened hold, the child twisted and strained feebly from time to time, realizing the futility of serious struggling.

The truck moved into a largely deserted industrial area and pulled in front of a darkened building. A hanging sign read WESTSIDE GARAGE. The man driving stepped from the truck, opened the garage door, drove in and then closed it again. Pulling off the white uniform and slipping into dark pants and a jacket which were hanging on a nail, he peeled the mustache off and removed the glasses, putting them into his jacket pocket.

Opening the trunk of a Chevy sedan parked in the garage, he took out two license plates, a screwdriver and a socket wrench, switched the plates with those on the truck and threw the removed ones into the trunk. He peeled a pair of smoothly taped PERFECTION LAUNDRY signs from the sides of the truck, revealing EASTERN SHORES LAUNDRIES advertising. Crumpling the signs, he threw them into the trunk of the Chevy. Then he opened the back door of the truck and took the blindfolded child, holding him while his partner changed into street clothes and also removed glasses and mustache.

They tied the child's hands and feet together, put another large adhesive strip over his mouth and laid him in the trunk of the Chevy. After throwing the white uniforms and the sheets into the trunk, they closed it. The gray-haired man climbed into the Chevy, the other into the truck. Backing both out of the garage, they locked the door and drove slowly away. A sign in the garage window read: EFFECTIVE JULY 1, CLOSED UNTIL FURTHER NOTICE.

They drove to Eastern Shores Laundries and parked the truck in a line with several others standing perpendicular to a fence in the area behind the building. A man in a white uniform carrying a clipboard stood on a low platform at the rear of the building. He waved at the man climbing from the truck. "She all set now, Roy?"

"Like a clock, Mr. Raccio. Real sweet."

"OK, Roy. Enjoy your vacation. Don't stay away too long." He waved a greeting at the man driving the Chevy as Roy climbed in next to him.

The gray-haired man drove the car out of the lot and back onto the street. "That couldn't have worked out better," he commented to Roy. "More'n I coulda hoped for. In fact, perfect."

"Yeah. I hoped he'd be back there standing around."

Driving at carefully controlled speed, they moved out of the city to a small house on the fringe of a sparsely built-up suburb. They pulled into a basement garage, and Roy lifted the boy out with an arm around his waist, carrying him like a blanket roll. They went upstairs into the house, down the center hall and into a bedroom.

"This kid don't weigh forty pounds," Roy said. He dropped the child, still bound, onto a steel-posted bed.

"Yeah, he's a puny kid."

"It was easy," Roy said. "Just as easy as you laid out. Christ, I can't get over it. Easy!"

"We haven't got to the hard part yet."

"This was the tricky part. We're out of sight the rest of the way."

"Let's do something with the kid."

"Leave him."

"We're gonna be here for a while. He can't stay like that." The gray-haired man walked over to the bed and sat down next to the thin child, who lay lashed hands to feet, his eyes and mouth taped. He took the child's shoulder in his hand. "If we let up on you, boy, you gonna behave yourself and do as you're told?"

8

The child made no attempt to nod or communicate but lay there, struggling to breathe through his nose over the tightly taped mouth.

"Leave him, Harry. Let him stay that way a-while."

Harry snapped his head around and scowled at Roy. "Idiot!" he whispered. Then he looked back down at the boy. "We'll take it easy with you if you don't give us any trouble, kid. You listening?"

The boy still did not move or attempt to communicate as he strained for each breath.

Harry glared at Roy again. He got up and walked across the room to a small desk, fished a pair of police handcuffs from a lower drawer and returned to the bed. Laying the handcuffs aside, he began loosening the tape on the child's mouth, finally removing it with a yank that made the child cry out.

After the tape was off, leaving his pink face reddened, the child began breathing through his mouth, sucking air down in noisy, rattling gulps. He was still lying on his side, his eyes taped, his wrists and ankles tied together. "I—I need my nebulizer," he said.

"What's he talking about?" Harry asked. "You got any idea?"

"How the hell would I know?"

"I need my nebulizer," the boy repeated. "It's in my pocket." The air whistled in and out of his mouth as he heaved with each breath.

"What are you talking about, boy?" Harry asked.

"My nebulizer. It's in my pocket. I have a respiratory problem."

Harry felt the boy's front pants pockets. He worked his thick fingers into one of them and brought out a complex plastic bottlelike object. "This what you're talking about?"

"That's it," the child said. A tear choked his voice, and his breathing became more labored. "I have to have my hands free."

"Leave him the hell alone," Roy said. "He'll quiet down if you just leave him alone. You stick it in his nose for him."

Harry untied the link of rope that lashed hands and feet together, and the boy uncoiled. Then he untied the foot-bindings. Snapping one side of the handcuffs around one of the boy's thin ankles, he tested it to make sure it couldn't come over his foot. Then he circled the other cuff around one metal post at the foot of the bed, locked it around the other ankle and began untying the boy's hands.

The child quickly pushed himself upright and felt around on the bed for the plastic device. Finding it, he picked it up, twisted here and there at it and stuck the end of the long neck in his mouth. He began caressing the bottle as he took a deep breath. He was deft with the device, the tape on his eyes no handicap.

"What the hell's he doing?" Roy said.

"The kid's got some kind of asthma. He's not too healthy. I told you that before."

"That's what we need. A sick one. What if

10

something happens to him before we get the money?"

"We've got to keep him in decent shape in case we need him on the phone."

The two men watched the boy as he continued working with the little plastic bottle. He tried a breath or two without it, a small one with it, two or three without, another with, several without, another with, a minute or two without it, a breath with it, and finally, twisting the top, he stuffed it back in his pocket. His breathing was quieter but not completely clear. Turning his head toward the men, he was visibly trembling. "I have to go to the bathroom." His voice was almost choked up again.

"Oh, Jesus," Roy snapped impatiently.

"It's all right," Harry said to the child. "You're human. You're allowed to go. We'll let you go when you have to." He walked to the desk and fished a small key on a string out of the drawer that had contained the handcuffs. He unlocked one side. "OK, kid, let's go." Helping the boy off the bed, he began leading him toward a bathroom off the hall outside the bedroom.

The child moved slowly, dragging the handcuff on his foot. Holding his arms out helplessly, he let Harry lead him into the bathroom and position him in front of the toilet, moving him closer so that his knees touched. He looked up at Harry as though he could see through the tape.

"It's OK," Harry said. "You don't have to close the door. No girls in this house."

The child, clumsy because of his taped eyes, fumbled with his clothes and finally relieved himself. He zipped himself as Harry flushed the toilet.

"Back on the bed. Let's go," Harry said, leading him back.

The boy walked slowly to the bed, moving with extended arms, like the blind. Harry pushed him into a sitting position.

"Up with the tootsies," Harry said as he re-shakled him to the bed.

"What are you men going to do?"

"Nothing, kid. Go to sleep," Roy snapped.

"But it's not time to go to sleep. It's afternoon," the child said.

"Just take it easy, kid," Harry said. He nodded to Roy to follow him into the hall. "You stupid bastard!" he said in a half whisper. "You called me by my name in there."

"Crissakes, Banner, you're treating that kid like he was your own!"

"Wise up, will ya, Roy! And keep your goddamn voice down. I told you we gotta keep the kid in good shape in case we need him on the phone. . . . It's time to make the first call. Go make the call. And, Jesus, take it easy."

"I'm just getting nervous. Now that we grabbed him, our neck is out. I wanta get the money, get rid of the kid and clear the hell out."

"Well, the first step is to make the call. Now don't forget. The first call is from the booth on Route Forty-six near the tracks. We been over what to say. Be sure you ask for both of 'em."

"You're telling me what to say?" Roy said. "Don't tell me what to say or do. You want to make the call?"

"You know we stick to the book. Now go make the call. Make sure you got change. And pick up some milk."

Roy studied Harry for a moment with a look that was quizzical and then slightly contemptuous. He turned and walked down the hall to the basement door, opened it and went slowly down the steps.

2

"Let me speak to Mr. Feldman."

"He not here."

"Let me speak to Mrs. Feldman."

"She not here either."

"When will Mr. Feldman be back?"

"I don't know. He out of town."

"When will Mrs. Feldman be back?"

"She not due for three weeks. She in Europe."

"Now you listen to me. You get in touch with Feldman. Tell him to come home. I'll call back tomorrow. Tell him if he ever wants to see his redheaded kid alive again, he'll be there when I call. And he. . . ."

"Hello? Who's this? Hello? What are you talking about? Gary right here in this house."

"The kid is not there. He's with me. Now, if Feldman wants to see him alive again, he'll do as I say. Tell him to get home. And he won't call the police. That clear? *No police!*"

"Gary right here in this house. *Gary*? Who is this?"

Roy hung up.

3

"Is this Mr. Victor Feldman?"

"Yes, it is."

"Go ahead, please."

"Hello, Victor?"

"Fred. What is it?" Feldman pulled himself up to a sitting position on the edge of the bed. He reached for a towel and dropped it over his nakedness.

"You'd better sit down, Victor."

"Don't tell me to sit down. Now, what is it?"

"You know I wouldn't call you there if it wasn't very important. I think you ought to sit down."

"Fred, my patience is wearing a little thin."

"I don't know how to say it except to say it. Victor . . . your little boy has been kidnapped."

"Gary? *My son, Gary? I can't—*" Then, with complete control: "Are you certain of this, Fred?"

"I'm afraid I am, Victor. Sara called me. She said she received a phone call. She didn't even know your boy was not there when the call came.

She said the man said if you want him alive, you should get home and not contact the police. He said he'd phone again tomorrow."

"Have you contacted the police, Fred?"

"All I've done is call you."

"Stay away from the police, Fred. Don't do anything. I'll catch a plane out tonight. I should be there by midnight. Maybe sooner. And I'll handle everything. It's best you keep a lid on this, do you understand?"

"I think we should get in touch with the police, Victor. The police, the FBI—frankly, Victor, I think you should welcome all the help you can get."

"Fred, you will do as I say."

"Is there *anything* you would like me to do now?" Fred's tone was restrained.

"Stay near the phone. I'll be back to you shortly. I'll want you to meet me. Everything clear?" He hung up.

"What was all the talk about police about?" asked the woman in the room.

"I'm going to have to catch a plane back home. Please handle canceling dinner and all our arrangements. And most important, don't repeat what you heard here tonight. Perhaps you'd better take a different plane back. A later flight."

"Of course. But what was all the police business?"

"Gary's been kidnapped."

"My God!"

Feldman picked up the phone and asked for an

16

overseas operator. While waiting, he covered the mouthpiece and turned. "Wait. Please don't get dressed yet."

She turned quickly and studied him with a questioning stare. "Victor—"

"Please." He sounded pained. "You know me well enough to know— Besides, there's nothing more I can do at this moment. . . . Uh, hello, operator? A credit card call, please. Just a moment." He covered the mouthpiece and turned to his companion. Pointing at his suit jacket in the closet: "Hand me the billfold from my inside coat pocket." He uncovered the phone. "One second, operator, and I'll give you all the information for the call." He took the billfold and opened it to the note pad inside. "Yes, here we are. I'd like to call Paris, France, Mrs. Victor Feldman. . . ." He studied the contours of the woman's naked back as he spoke into the phone.

"Is this Mrs. Victor Feldman?"

"Hello? Uh, yes, speaking. Hello?"

"Here's your party, sir."

"Isobel?"

"Is that you, Victor? My lord, what on earth—"

"Isobel, Gary's been kidnapped."

"Victor, I can't understand you. There's such a mob here. We just got in from the loveliest show and we're having a late party. Guess who showed up here in Paris tonight?"

"I'm glad you're enjoying yourself. Gary's been kidnapped."

"Victor, I can't understand you. There must be thirty people here."

"Tell them to shut up!"

"Victor, I can't understand you. Could you shout? Wait. I'll take the phone in the bedroom."

"Gary has been kidnapped!"

"Victor, what are you saying? I must have misunderstood you. Wait, let me get the other phone."

"Gary has been kidnapped! Tell your friends to shut up!"

She placed her hand over the mouthpiece, and when she removed it, the background noise had subsided. "Victor, what did you say?"

"Gary has been kidnapped."

"Is this your idea of something funny?"

"Does it sound like my sense of humor?"

"Victor? Are you serious?"

"Goddammit! Of course I'm serious!"

"Victor, that child will perish without his medication. Get in touch with George Berman and—"

"What good is a doctor when we don't know where Gary is? I just called to see if you would like to come home."

"George can talk to the kidnappers and tell them about Gary's medication. Of course I'll come home. As soon as I can get there. It means canceling a few things, that's all. I'll see what flight I can get."

"What did you say?"

"I'll get there as quickly as I can."

"Tell your friends there not to leak the word

back. I'm not calling the police yet. Is that absolutely clear?"

"Are you at home now?"

"I'm in Pittsburgh. Fred called me."

"I'll see you at home as soon as I can."

4

Roy had been gone for about thirty minutes. The boy was lying still on the bed, his feet shackled, the handcuffs restricting his movement to the point that his positions on the bed were limited and uncomfortable. Harry sat by a curtained window, looking out. A small radio on a table in front of the window was tuned to a local station, broadcasting rock-and-roll music and a chattering disc jockey. The periodic news breaks made no mention of the kidnapping.

Harry walked over and looked down at the boy who was lying motionless on the bed. "You hungry?" He bumped the mattress with his knee.

The boy shook his head slowly.

"Why not?"

The boy shrugged his shoulders and twisted up his mouth as if he might cry, as if he hated being asked that question.

"You're kinda puny. You oughta eat more. How old are you, anyway?"

20

"Eight." His voice was slightly tear-locked, his breathing a trace wheezy.

"Eight? You look six."

"I'm small for my age."

"I figured you were older than you look. You talk a little too good for someone as little as you."

"I haven't said very much. How can you tell?"

"I can tell. . . . Where'd you get such red hair? That's the reddest hair I ever saw."

The boy didn't answer. He was still choked up and wheezing. He sat up, took the plastic device from his pocket, manipulated it and drew in one breath of mist.

"Do you have to use that thing every time somebody talks to you about anything?"

"Why did you bring me here? What are you going to do?"

"We're just going to keep you here with us for a while."

"And then, what? Take me home?"

"Now just take it easy, Redhead. . . . What's your name, anyway?"

"Gary."

"Gary? What are you, a movie star? I think I like Redhead better. Gary? Jesus! Gary!"

"If my name's so funny, what's yours?"

"It's—" Harry hesitated. "Just call me, hey, mister."

"I already know your name."

Harry grabbed the child abruptly by the arm. "You what?"

The child jumped at the harsh, unexpected grip. He didn't answer.

"What did you say about knowing my name?" Harry was almost shouting at the child. He felt the color drain from his face and a layer of perspiration form on his upper lip.

The child hunched his shoulders. "I was only kidding."

Harry eased his grip, trying to make it seem more a friendly grip. He squeezed the child's shoulder. "You had me worried, Redhead. I was afraid you'd been listening when you should have been relaxing. I was afraid you'd been listening a little too much, you know that?" He heard a car in the driveway. "Sometimes it's better not to hear too much." He walked out of the bedroom and into the hall to meet Roy coming up the steps. "You make the call?"

"It was just like you said. Neither of them there. I talked to the nigger that does the cooking."

"Give her the message, like we had planned?"

"Yeah. She was surprised as hell. She didn't know the kid wasn't there. She said Feldman's out of town and the kid's mother's in Europe. Jesus!" Roy laugh-grunted. "Guess maybe we're gonna make this a trip for 'em both to remember. Told the nigger to get Feldman home and to stay the hell away from the cops. Told her I'd call Feldman tomorrow. Hell, I could've made the call from here."

Harry rubbed himself on the back of the neck. "Hope this doesn't take longer than I'd planned. The kid just gave me a scare. I thought he knew my name. We gotta watch using names in front

22

of him. That could make things different. . . . Is that the milk in that bag?"

"This is my milk. Christ, I wish you'd quit worrying about that lousy kid. Why don't we get rid of him now and not have to worry about him any more? Little sick bastard. We'll put him out of his misery." Roy walked into the kitchen and set the bag down on the counter. Lifting two fifths of whiskey from the bag, he twisted the second one open, poured some into a glass, took a little. "Want a drink?"

"Roy, I didn't figure on killing the kid or anyone else, and I still don't. We don't kill, and we don't cross state lines. Just take a little money. The kid's never seen us, and he don't know where he is."

"Harry, I know what you said, and you're stupid. With the kid gone, we're free. He's the only one knows anything about us."

"We may need him on the phone. For the time being we gotta make things as easy as we can."

"For the time being," Roy answered.

"We might as well try and keep the kid happy for now. It'll work in our favor to keep the kid as cheerful as we can."

"How'd I ever get talked into this with you for a partner?" Roy said, shaking his head.

"Who worked this whole thing out?"

"What'd you lay it out for if you didn't have guts enough to pull it off?"

"Will you please leave the planning to me? There's a nice, neat, well-planned way to do everything, and that's the way we got the best chance of pulling it off. I don't like the idea of killing that sick little kid off. Him, or nobody else, for that matter. And I don't think we have to do it. We leave him and things'll cool quick. We kill him and, Christ, they'll never stop looking for us."

Roy picked up the bottle and splashed more whiskey into the glass. Taking a mouthful, he stared intently at Harry as he got it down. "I don't care what you don't like, Harry. As soon as I get my hands on the money, I'm getting rid of that kid. I don't care how I do it, pal. I'll do it any nice painless way you like. But I'm not leaving no living witness now. Not the way things have gone so easy."

"We've got a way to go before we get the money. For the time being we'll keep with the book. . . . We need some milk. We got everything else. . . . Christ, I can't figure how I forgot milk. Get a couple cartons. . . . And why don'cha get a couple decks of cards? Kidnappers always sit around playing cards."

Roy drained the glass and set it on the counter. "Don't monkey, Harry. Don't monkey." Walking out of the kitchen and into the hall, he went slowly down the steps toward the basement, landing with emphasis on each step.

After Harry heard the car's engine start up, he took a glass from the counter, measured a healthy slug of whiskey into it, added a little tap water and took a long swallow.

24

5

Roy returned in thirty minutes with a brown paper sack containing two quart cartons of milk and a small flat white bag. Walking into the kitchen, he set the milk down and drew a deck of cards out of the small bag, tossing it so it slid a few feet along the counter. He picked up the whiskey and the glass he had used before and poured himself another drink. "You fixing something to eat?"

Harry was standing by the white enamel stove, his hand on the oven handle. He periodically pulled it open and glanced inside. "Fried chicken, pal, just like Mother used to make. Right out of the freezer, according to the book. Tomorrow, roast beef. There's some beer cold. We can sit down and have a small dinner party."

"You gonna bring the kid to the table like one of the family or serve him in bed like Prince Charming?" Roy asked. The high-pitched chirp of his voice seemed almost ludicrous in contrast with the granite undertone of his sarcasm.

"We'll eat, and then I'll take him something in

there. These are almost ready. Get out a couple beers and open 'em."

They sat at the enamel-top table and ate without speaking, drinking beer out of the bottles. Roy held chicken in his left hand and forked peas and mashed potatoes with his right hand, dropping his fork into the food in the aluminum tray to pick up his beer or wad up a slice of bread. Harry held bread in his left, using his right for chicken, the beer bottle or the fork.

Harry had known Roy for about a year. Roy owned the Westside Garage, and Harry had come on to Roy by taking a job in Roy's garage after his last stretch in prison. Harry had been in the infantry during World War II and was among the myriad frustrated dogfaces trying to find lives for themselves as they were mustered out. He took a job in an aircraft plant on Long Island and was content for a while. He married a waitress, Rose, who was a good sturdy little citizen. They bought a little house in a row of little houses on the island. With the unexpected suddenness that such things happen, he lost the job in the come-and-go of government contracts. While he was looking for work, Rose had to go back to work. They had had no children. During his search, he was led into feeling highly encouraged about a halfway promising job with an automobile assembly plant in Jersey, and he hitched his hopes to it.

When the job fell through, Harry took to drinking with an old Army buddy he ran across whose name was Len Bartow. Bartow was fed up with looking for jobs that were "all lifting and hauling and no payday to amount to anything." He goaded Harry into joining him in breaking and entering a service station, then another. Harry was able to work on these with Bartow without Rose's knowing because she was working a late shift. Things went so well Harry and Bartow decided to upgrade themselves from breaking and entering to armed robbery. Their first attempt was a neat success. They tried and scored again and then again.

It became tougher and tougher for Harry not to expose the money he had been accumulating to Rose. He was proud of his handiwork. Every job had been a good clean job. He began to develop a mental image of himself: Don't hurt anybody; just take a little money. It was harmless enough. Money was insured. He developed a kind of humor in his own mind about what he thought of as his new career: pleasant working conditions, no interruptions, short hours and good pay.

He knew Rose wouldn't buy his unemployment indefinitely, and he figured she would soon begin to question how someone who was unemployed could seem so self-satisfied and preoccupied. It was getting harder and harder to sound convincing with lies about the heartache of knocking on doors and being turned away. He finally decided to take any kind of job as a front for Rose. It would give him an excuse to bring home some of the money. He got on as a hand pumping gas at the service station which had been their first mark. With a big grin he told

Bartow he felt better working someplace where he already knew his way around.

He started earning thirty a week and bringing home seventy-five to a hundred. This seemed pretty good pay to Rose for pumping gas, better in fact by a good margin than the take-home from the aircraft plant. He explained it away by saying he was like an assistant manager, running the place a good part of the time. This might easily have come to be the truth as the owner liked him for his sense of humor, dependability and air of responsibility. He gave Harry a ten-dollar raise a short while after Harry came there, and Harry momentarily considered going to him with a serious proposition. But Harry abandoned the idea to concentrate on his career.

The money he was bringing home was good enough that he was easily able to convince Rose to stay home and quit her waiting tables and her lousy hours. He wanted her to be a lady. He continued with his new career, working with Bartow, going out occasionally at night "to get together with his old Army buddies for a couple drinks," and particularly on weekends on "fishing trips." After a hard week of work he was entitled to a little relaxation. "Bartow has all the gear in his car," he would explain, and he enjoyed this because it wasn't far from the truth. A problem arose one day when Rose decided she'd like to go fishing with them. He and Bartow had to buy equipment, get some directions and try to make it look as if they knew what they were doing. They explained their unfamiliarity with the area they went to on the basis that this was their first visit to this new, highly recommended area. "First time we been here, sweetheart. The place we usually go ain't fit for you." Fortunately, the weather turned sour, and getting good and wet ended her interest. She knew nothing about fishing and didn't notice that they knew no more than she.

Harry and his partner became proficient at their work. They wouldn't consider big jobs, like banks. They stuck to "peanut stores." They developed almost a sixth sense for spotting when a service station, small shop, restaurant or the like was perfect for a "night call" or a "personal visit." They favored package stores and pawnshops. Harry considered these fringe areas which made money feeding on people's problems. Their sixth sense extended to cars. They could almost smell a car with the keys in it a block away. They hated having to bother to jump the ignition. Harry said it was too much like stealing. They could watch people get out of cars and tell whether they had left the keys and how long they'd be gone. They lined up outlets where they could turn over the ones they picked up and even did some shopping around to get the best price.

Harry was content with life. There had been few even slightly close calls on their "fishing trips." They went often enough to satisfy themselves and seldom enough to avoid arousing Rose's suspicion. Rose was a lady. Though still childless, she made Harry a fine home.

Things continued to go smoothly along until the day a wiry little pawnbroker decided to argue

with Bartow and Bartow got impatient and hit
the little man in the head with the barrel of his
gun. Harry didn't like this. Guns were to threaten
people, to persuade people. Guns were not to hurt
people. The way he had it figured, it wasn't necessary to hurt people to take a little money off them.
Money was only money. It was usually insured,
and you lose what you have today, more comes in
tomorrow. Harry didn't like the sight of the little
man lying on the floor, bleeding from an ugly
hole in his head. This put a new dimension on
things, a new charge on the list of charges against
them. It hadn't been a real emergency. It hadn't
called for emergency tactics.

He and Len lost their composure when this
happened. They hurriedly cleaned the register and
ran out of the shop, guns in their hands, looking
around. Usually they intimidated whomever they
held up, under threat of a return visit, to do
nothing for five, or ten, or thirty minutes, depend-
ing on the victim's gullibility, and then walked
calmly to their car and drove away. This time
someone spotted them in their frantic gunslinging
withdrawal, and the police were quickly after
them. They piled up their car in the chase, and
Bartow was knocked unconscious. Harry made
it away, but he was not totally surprised when
the police came to pick him up to go downtown
the following night.

Rose was crushed by Harry's conviction. She
had insisted on his innocence until it became
obvious there was no mistake. She was the last
to know. Shortly after Harry heard the bars clang

shut behind him, he heard from Rose that she was leaving him.

The years spent inside dampened Harry's ardor for his career. His countenance took on a kind of sadness, a resigned, fateful outlook. His humorous reflections were less humorous and less frequent. His Rose divorced him and remarried. When he finally emerged, he was determined not to resume his career. He took job after job, mostly as an auto mechanic, resisting the urge to pick up a car or tap some small, quiet service station. But things looked too green on the shady side of the street, and he started back by picking up an easy car. Working alone, he broke into a couple of small shops. Then he broke into a service station one night only to find that he had selected carelessly and hadn't really broken in. The owner was still on the premises. Harry lost a fistfight and heard the reverberating clang for the second time, this time with an aching jaw. During his second stay out of traffic, he spent his hours of contemplation going down an entirely different avenue. He resolved to leave career opportunities alone. That is, unless the stake made it irresistible. He decided his approach was wrong. One carefully planned big job was the only way. Go for broke and then get out. He was a fool to stick his neck out over and over for penny-ante stuff. It was time to either use his head or leave it alone. The key word was planning, careful, detailed, checked and rechecked planning.

He got out and went back to being an auto mechanic. He reestablished contact with a kid sister, June, whom he'd hardly known in recent years, particularly since he had spent so much of them away. She was around twenty-nine, maybe thirty, he figured. She had just gotten in and out of a bad marriage, and perhaps this made her wiser and more sympathetic to his situation. She was an attractive girl, bright, aggressive, ambitious; she had as much class as a girl could acquire without background and schooling. She lived alone and was an executive secretary to the president of a large importing company in New York. From time to time she had Harry over for a meal at her flat in the city. She would tell him about her work, and he would reminisce about his golden era with Rose.

Harry didn't like his first connection as an auto mechanic. The owner was so skeptical of Harry's police history he watched him obsessively, and this got to be "a real pain in the ass" in a hurry. Harry quit and looked for another job.

He found Roy Walls, who owned the Westside Garage. Roy couldn't care less about Harry's past. Harry had a halfway decent pair of hands, and that was all Roy cared about. Roy didn't worry much about not being able to handle anyone who worked for him. Despite a birdsong voice, Roy had a rock-hardness about him that was evident in his manner of saying and doing things. A veteran of the Korean War, he'd rather enjoyed it because he liked to kill. He got a boot out of the way a single well-placed bullet would drop a man. He sometimes commented that the end of the war took his toys away. He came back, opened a

32

garage and did reasonably well at it. He never married because "wives screw up a man's social life," which included drinking and hunting, his killing outlet.

As Harry made his occasional visits with his sister, June, an idea began to form in his mind. Her boss was worth a large fortune and had only one child. Kidnapping was a far-out idea, in fact, a totally new ball game from anything he knew and very, very risky business. But the payday was there. Perhaps with enough planning it could be pulled off. The more he got together with her, and the more she talked about her boss, the more he ruminated about the possibilities. It could be simple, harmless and that one big payday. He was extremely cautious about not letting her pick up his line of thought, even when he pumped her for details. He made a science of questioning her. His mind became totally involved with the possibilities. He became more intrigued with each passing day. And more confident.

From time to time, when Harry and Roy went out for a couple of drinks, Roy would taunt Harry about the nickle-and-dime crook he used to be. Harry would take it well and allude to some future date when he was going to go flat out and pick up a king's ransom on one quick job and retire from the grease pit. "When you get it all worked out so that nothing can go wrong, tell me about it and maybe I'll help you," Roy often said in his bird tones. And he would add, "But it's gotta be perfect, or don't waste my time."

After a while Roy began developing a strong

curiosity about the idiot notion Harry had, and
Harry would put him off with: "It's not perfect
yet. Let's talk about something else." Occasionally
Roy became insistent, and Harry's evasions only
inflamed his curiosity. Finally, Roy reached the
red-necked stage, and Harry briefly laid it out for
him. Roy then dismissed the whole thing with a
"you're out of your goddamn head" attitude, and
Harry moved back to the offensive, talking in
hundreds of thousands of tax-free dollars for a
couple of days' work and "nobody none the worse
for it."

Harry continued picking away at Roy until Roy
began to react in a half-serious way as Harry discussed one detail or another. "We've even got a
supply of laundry trucks at our disposal, anytime
we want them," Harry said one day, from under
a laundry truck. Roy had a maintenance contract
with a large laundry for their entire fleet of trucks.

"These trucks can be traced to me," Roy
snapped.

"We use stolen plates and tape phony signs
on the side of the truck," Harry answered. "Somebody comes to the door, you came to pick up the
dirty clothes. So it's the wrong house. You ask for
directions. It's that simple. We even plan in
advance what address you ask about. We plan
every detail with changes for anything that can
happen. I even thought about what you do if
they give you their laundry. You take it."

As more time went by, they planned detail on
top of detail, even though Roy had by no means
committed himself to taking the idea seriously.

But planning it and trying to guess what unexpected situations might develop became a preoccupation when they were sitting around having a couple of drinks and even a distraction around the shop.

Harry doted on his sister's invitations, encouraging her to invite him more and more often so he could soak up in-depth information about her boss. "Jesus, I just don't understand," Harry said to her on one occasion. "The more you tell me about him, the more he seems like a real gold-plated SOB. And yet you sound like you half appreciate the guy."

She paused as if not knowing quite how to answer. "It's really a very good job, and he's quite square with me. He's, he's not, well, he's not a bad man. He's just very shrewd in business."

"And you say he's away most of the time in one direction and his old lady's away in another?"

"She takes trips to Europe and the Caribbean and such for months on end."

"And you make all their reservations, wherever they go?"

"That's what an executive secretary is for."

"And who did you say takes care o' their kid?"

"The two maids . . . and the doctor, if anything comes up . . . and the various tutors that come to the house. They have him tutored at home instead of sending him to school."

Harry fed this new information into their planning the next day. "It's shaping up, Roy. Things are falling into place like tumblers. The vault's gonna be opening soon."

Roy was beginning to half smile when he reflected on prospects for pulling it off. It was stalking, even if it wasn't killing.

"Tell you what let's do, Roy," Harry said one day. "Let's go to their house and look it over. I'm gonna show you something. I been there once already."

They drove to the Feldman house one afternoon. Harry, at the wheel, pulled the car up to the door under the archway as if he lived there. Climbing out of the car, he walked in the front door of the house, beckoning to Roy to follow him. They stood in the large foyer, looking the place over like prospective buyers. The only sound was a radio playing somewhere toward the back of the first floor. Suddenly a small, frail redheaded boy walked out of the rooms off the large foyer, glanced at them without reaction and then walked up the wide stairway to the second floor. Roy bristled, and his eyes took on a hunter's stony concentration.

"We shoulda grabbed him then," Roy said as they drove away.

"We gotta plan every detail," Harry said. "Every detail down to the last detail. Planning. Understand? Planning. We make a book and we go by it. Every angle covered."

Harry became studious in his planning. He hardly did any work around the shop. He was always writing something, making a list of one thing or another, or marking the big city map with a green felt-tip pen. "Green's my favorite color," he'd say as he indicated a likely phone booth.

They drove around the area of the Feldman home repeatedly, studying the least noticed routes away from it. They selected a hard-to-find road nearby, Fernhill Drive, which they would ask for if confronted with a situation in which they would have to explain their presence at the Feldman house. If necessary, they would explain two men in the laundry truck by saying Harry was being transferred to a new route and he was breaking Roy in on his route. "It's not what you say that's important," Harry lectured. "It's thinking about it enough and practicing it enough that when comes time to say it, you say it easy and it sounds natural and right."

Harry spent a lot of time calling travel agencies, getting facts on where they might go without passports or other identifying papers. The travel agents didn't cheer him up much. If he was going to keep the thing clean of likely pitfalls, there weren't any really easy ways out. Things were pretty well bottled up. He didn't want to sweat phony passports. He knew nothing about such things. He had no idea how to even start looking for phony passports. Although his many meticulously careful phone conversations with many different travel agents had provided him with a superficial instant sophistication about air travel to resort areas, it hadn't helped him with the painful fact that he couldn't put his hands on suitable nonidentifying identification papers.

As he pondered this problem, he became more and more convinced that he had better stick to domestic flight patterns, at least initially. He finally selected a pattern and began to detail it with actual flight numbers. They would leave the boy bound and gagged where he'd be found the next morning, drive to Kennedy and fly west. They would fly to San Francisco because this gave them a number of flights out of New York to select from. In order to cover the eventuality of timing mishaps, they would make multiple reservations, all under different names, and keep a careful list so that whenever they arrived at the airport, they would refer to the list and see who they were and what flight they were on. From San Francisco they would head north to Washington State, flying to Seattle. From this point they would go on an extended hunting vacation, an aspect of the plan Roy seemed at times more interested in than the kidnap and the money.

During negotiations with the parents, they would use a piece of vacant property Roy owned but didn't live in because it was too far from the garage. It was a small cheap one-family house, fairly well obscured in small grubby trees and undergrowth and removed from other houses in the vicinity. "Jesus, this place is too good to be true" was Harry's reaction. The house was one of the major simplifying factors in Harry's planning.

When July 1 rolled around, they began their preliminaries. Harry was satisfied with the completeness of his "book." He checked out of his rooming house to go on a hunting vacation. "Going down to the Smokies," he told the landlady. "If I like it enough, who knows when I'll be back! Maybe never. Got no real ties here." Roy also checked out of his small flat, and they moved into Roy's house. They had the phone reconnected under the name of the last tenant, Esposito. The sign stating the garage would be closed had been in the window for more than three weeks. Roy advised the laundry they could keep their maintenance commitments only through that week. This provided the one truck required. Mrs. Feldman was in Europe. They would grab the child on Thursday, negotiate on Friday, pick up the money on Saturday and fly out on Saturday night.

On the Fourth of July the two of them went on a drinking spree, spending hour after hour tangling with waves of doubts and fears. Harry was satisfied with the book but still subject to spates of indecisiveness. He and Roy took turns playing hawk and dove as they drank, each prodding and needling the other. They finally made their way back to the house. They had one last pint of whiskey, which they finished between them before passing out. They slept through most of the next day, Wednesday, and when they finally got up, during late afternoon, Roy was coldly and soberly resolute in his intention of carrying out the plan. Harry, too, had come out of his stupor in a positive frame of mind. They would make the pickup on the following day, Thursday, as laid out in the book.

Roy scrubbed the mashed potato compartment

of his tray with a wadded slice of bread and stuffed it into his mouth, washing it down with the last of his beer. "Go feed your kid now." He wiped his face on his upper sleeve.

"I'll do that," Harry answered. "The book says that while I'm doing that, you go burn the laundry truck signs and get rid of the two plates."

Roy smiled an ugly smile. "Think I'll nail the two plates on the garage wall. That's what you do with old plates, isn't it?"

"Those ain't old. They're so hot they'll burn the place down. Bury 'em like the book says. Where they won't be found."

"You just go feed your baby."

6

"How about something to eat, Redhead?" Harry walked over to the bed carrying a chicken TV dinner and a small glass of milk. A piece of plain white bread lay across the top of the food. The child was sprawled limply back on the bed. He glanced at the bandage around the child's face and noticed that the bottom edge was loosened just below the eyes. "Redhead, you been monkeying with that bandage? I don't want you monkeying with that bandage or we'll shave off that red hair and tape up your whole head. Understand? I just left your hands free so you could use your medicine. Want your hands tied?" He moved to the desk, put the food down, opened a drawer and fished out a roll of wide adhesive tape. He peeled a strip a foot long, notched the tape with his teeth, tore it off and placed it diagonally over the child's eye, on top of the bandage already there, so that the new strip extended from the hairline on his forehead down across his face to the neck below his ear. He rubbed and pressed the tape so roughly to seal it that the child whimpered several times. Harry peeled another foot of tape and placed it over the other eye, forming a big X that almost covered the child's embryonic hooknose. "Now don't monkey with the tape anymore, Redhead."

"You don't have to hurt me," the child answered in a bruised voice.

"I didn't try to hurt you. I just don't want you to see anything for a while. Now, how about a little something to eat?" Harry returned the tape to the desk drawer.

"I feel almost like I'm at home," the child said in a still-bruised tone. "That's all anybody ever says to me. You've got to eat."

"It's time, Redhead. You gotta eat. I fixed you a nice chicken dinner."

"I can't eat chicken. I'm allergic to chicken."

Harry looked down at the small aluminum tray. "Whatta ya mean, allergic to it? This is a nice fried chicken dinner."

The boy twisted his mouth into a curl of resigned indifference. "Whenever I eat any poultry product, chicken or eggs or anything containing them, I get sick and swell up and develop a rash and start wheezing."

"Well, you gotta eat something. There's other things here besides the chicken. I'll eat the chicken, and you eat the rest of it."

"I'm not hungry." The child choked up. "Besides, I can't eat if I can't see."

"I'm gonna feed it to ya. There's potatuhs, peas, bread and a glass of milk."

"I don't like peas."

"You oughta eat everything."

"That's all I hear at home. From everybody."

Harry picked up the slice of bread and put it in the boy's hand. "Here, hold the bread and I'll feed you the potatuhs. You gotta eat something." He took a small forkful of mashed potatoes and held it to the small mouth. Although the child didn't accept the bite with much interest, he did accept it. Feeding him gave Harry a vague pleasurable sensation, a kind of warming satisfaction. He was helping a helpless child, something he had never done before. He was feeding an invalid. He was leading the blind. "Here you go," he said as he brought up a second forkful and touched it to the small lips. He watched intently as the child opened his mouth and listened to the nearly inaudible sound of swallowing. He brought up another forkful and then another.

The boy balked after five or six small forkfuls. "I don't want any more."

"Eat the bread."

"I don't want it." The boy tossed the bread aside on the bed.

"Here's some milk." Getting no negative reaction, Harry brought the milk up carefully to the child's lips. He did this best at holding the glass, but even with the child's help, a little spilled down the freckled chin. He daubed at it with his finger. He couldn't remember the last time he had touched a child's face. He touched again just for the curious sensation of it.

The boy stopped drinking after about half the

small glass. "I don't want any more." He pushed away the glass.

"Two bites o' potatuh and a haffa glass o' milk. Jesus. No wonder you're such a shrimp." Harry leaned over and set the milk on the floor. Then he picked up a chicken leg and bit into it. He reached out, grabbed the neck of the boy's polo shirt and pulled it up to wipe the milk off his chin.

"Hey! What are you doing? Didn't you bring me a napkin?"

"I'll bring you a beach towel next time. Tomorrow you get roast beef. How does that sound?" He dropped the cleaned chicken leg and picked up a thigh.

"Do I get any dessert?"

"What kinda dessert?"

"I like all kinds of desserts, unless they have eggs in them."

Harry smiled at the blindfolded child, flashing a mouthful of chicken thigh. "When we get some money from your old man, maybe if we have time, we'll buy you something good. Maybe we'll get you an ice cream. Why don't you just flop back and take it easy for a while?"

The child shrugged his shoulders and let himself down flat on the bed. Harry picked up the glass, the bread and the tray and started out of the room. "Keep your mitts off the bandage or I'll shave your head. OK, Redhead?"

7

Fred Herbert could never have been an importer. He could never have been an entrepreneur of any kind. He wouldn't have known where or how to begin. He was incapable of starting anything, of setting anything into motion. But he had ambition and enough of a certain native smart to know that there was a rather high standard of living to be enjoyed by simply providing Victor Feldman with what he wanted and when he wanted it, before he wanted it, if possible.

Fred was a vice-president, the only vice-president, in Victor Feldman's firm. Fred's family enjoyed garden club circles because he made an art form of pleasing Victor Feldman. He was fifty-five, Feldman's senior by some ten years. He had been with "Victor" since the early years when "Victor" was creating his empire; now he brought a certain dignity to "Mr. Feldman's" firm, handling "Personnel," "Administrative Services," "Accounting," and similar functions. He gave Feldman's business a kind of corporate façade. But

Feldman still ran the business with a telephone, the way he had done since the day he left another importing firm to begin building his own empire and, subsequently, to merge with Isobel's family's business.

Fred waited quietly in the terminal, standing at the mouth of the red-carpeted portable passageway from Feldman's flight. He tried to smile at the scowling Feldman emerging from the passageway. "I've my car parked right in front. I felt it was the quickest, easiest way to get you home."

"This whole thing is preposterous. I'll see that they're castrated before they're hung."

"How was your flight? Did you have any trouble getting a seat?"

"I wasn't allowed to carry my bag on. I'll have to remember to use a smaller bag the next time my son is to be kidnapped."

"Baggage handling is quite fast nowadays."

"If it isn't damn fast, we won't wait. I can send for it. Is there any new information since we last spoke?"

"Nothing, I'm afraid." Fred was breathing hard keeping up with Feldman as they walked up the terrazzo corridor to the front of the terminal and down the escalator to the lower level.

Feldman eased his way to the front of the crowd surrounding the baggage discharge turntable. His bag was one of the first group to slide down onto the revolving surface. He leaned grabbed it and forced his way out of the crowd of others waiting. "This terminal is inadequately air-conditioned," he said to Fred as they left the terminal into the hot summer night. "I hope your car is in better shape."

"It's working very well."

They walked out to Fred's business car, which was an off-white four-door Continental. It was air-conditioned and equipped with a two-way radio. It was presumptuously parked in the drive in front of the terminal. It had a flat tire. "My Lord, I can't understand it," Fred said. "There was no indication that I was losing air on the way out here."

"Please, Fred," Feldman said impatiently, "which will be faster, getting this fixed or renting another car?"

"Surely we can get this changed. I have a spare."

Feldman pulled a money clip from his pocket and slipped out a twenty-dollar bill. "Get a porter to change it at once. If you can't get one in five minutes, rent an air-conditioned car, a large one. I'm going inside to the bar. I could use a drink."

"If I can't get the tire changed right away, what should I do about my car?" Fred didn't dare remark about the money.

"Let that be a police problem. It'll keep them off the streets. You can handle reclaiming the car by telephone tomorrow." Feldman left Fred standing by the car with the twenty in his hand and walked back into the terminal.

A few minutes later Fred approached Feldman, who was sitting in a booth in the darkened cocktail lounge. Feldman got up, dropped two bills on the table and led Fred out.

"I rented an air-conditioned Dodge."

"You couldn't find anyone to change yours?"

"No. The porters said to call some service which they said takes a little time."

"Did you offer them the entire twenty?"

Fred flushed. "Yes."

"Surprising you got no takers. You put my bag in?"

"Yes."

"Please drive. This the car?"

"Of course. Yes. I left a note for the police on my car."

Feldman grabbed Fred's arm as he was about to slip the key into the ignition. "What sort of note?" he asked.

"Just a note that said I was forced to leave the car because of a serious emergency and that I would reclaim the car tomorrow and pay any—"

"Go get the note. The note isn't necessary. It'll cost the same either way and I don't want to stir up anything."

"Yes. I see your point. Of course." Fred got out and went after the note. He was hailed by a policeman as he left his car, carrying the note. "I'm going for help, Officer. I won't leave it any longer than necessary," he answered in a raised voice. He felt his face flush with the lie as he spoke. He went back into the terminal and out a different door, back to the rental car, keeping an eye on the policeman. He climbed back in next to Feldman and started the car. "I have the note."

"Tomorrow morning I want you to get me fifty thousand dollars in small, unmarked bills, with out arousing any attention. Bring it to me at home."

Fred thought briefly about this as he drove. "How can I do that without arousing any attention? Fifty thousand is a lot of small bills."

"Oh, come, Fred. That should be your cup of tea. You're in charge of my accounting, my office. . . . I don't know how. That's what I pay you for. Go to a lot of different banks. Do it any way you want, but get it to me by noon tomorrow."

"I'll see that you have it," Fred answered quietly. He remained silent for a moment. "How can you be sure of the amount before you've talked to them?"

Feldman half laughed. "Well, I certainly won't offer it all to them. I'll see what they ask."

"I imagine they're going to ask more than that. What makes you think it will be enough?"

"My dear fellow, don't underestimate me."

Fred didn't comment and chose not to say anything more. He drove on in silence. He muttered dull one-word reactions to Feldman's occasional conversation about the kidnappers or office matters. Feldman finally became annoyed with this and lasped into a state of irritated quiet.

8

A dark sedan turned into Feldman's driveway seconds before Feldman and Fred entered it. As Fred brought the rented Dodge to a stop behind the other car, the two men in the front seat got out on opposite sides and walked back toward Feldman and Fred. They had the nondescript business suits and assured moves of obvious policemen. "Oh, hell, Fred, how did they find out?" Feldman snapped, watching the two men approach.

"Is either of you Victor Feldman?" asked the one who had not been driving.

"I'm Victor Feldman. Who are you?"

"I'm Lieutenant Ed Schamper from the city police department downtown. We are out checking on a call we received—"

"May I see some proof of your identity?"

"Why, certainly. Sorry," Schamper said with an easy smile. He drew a leather flap from his pants pocket and flashed a shield at Feldman. He started to put it back.

"May I examine it?"

Schamper's smile showed a trace of impatience as he drew the shield out again and handed it to Feldman.

"Thank you, Lieutenant. Now, what can I do for you?" Feldman returned the shield.

"We're out checking on a call we just received. A Mr. Bernard Friedlander called and said that you have a son who has been kidnapped."

"Why don't you go and arrest Barney Friedlander? This is a very unfunny practical joke."

"Do you have a son, Mr. Feldman?"

"Yes."

"May we see him?"

"He isn't home."

"Where is he?"

"He's visiting an aunt in Philadelphia."

"Is your wife at home, Mr. Feldman?"

"She's away."

"Could you tell us where?"

"Is there some reason why I have to answer these questions? I'm really very tired and do not wish to be a party to Barney Friedlander's distorted sense of humor."

"Mr. Feldman, Mr. Friedlander called and stated he received a call from his wife from Paris. He said his wife was with your wife when you called her and told her your boy had been taken."

"That's ridiculous. My boy is in Philadelphia visiting his aunt and having a wonderful time."

"May I have the name and address of this aunt in Philadelphia? In order to complete this investigation, false or not, we'll want to contact the police in Philadelphia and have them check on the child."

Feldman opened the car door and stepped out. He opened the back door and reached in for his suitcase. "Why don't you come into the house, Lieutenant?"

They went in, followed by Fred and the other policeman. They were met at the door by the fear-stricken cook and the other maid, who stood helplessly in her black uniform with the white apron and the white cap on her head. The two women had been standing by the door, watching the exchange in the driveway through the slender strip of cut glass next to the door.

"Mistuh Feldman?" said the cook. She paused, not knowing what she should say or do. "Did you hear any more from Gary?"

"No. Have you?"

She looked at the two strange men.

"It's all right. They're police, but they know."

"I told Mistuh Fred all the man said this evenin'."

"That's OK then. Get some ice, would you, Sara?"

The other maid, a striking, tall brown girl, continued to stand dumbly, waiting to be told what to do.

"Would you put my bag in my room, please, Janeeta."

She broke into a broad smile. "It will be all right, Mr. Feldman," she said in a melodic Jamaican-English singsong. "You will see. We will get

the little master back, and it will be all right."
She turned and walked away.

"One of my imports," Feldman said, smiling.
"I'm in the importing business, as you may know
if you've been investigating me." He led them
into a large paneled room. He opened a bar behind
foldaway panels at one end of the room. "A
drink, Lieutenant?"

"Thanks, no."

"Your partner's name?"

"Peseta."

"Mr. Peseta? Drink?"

Peseta had walked over to the glass tank containing the two tiny animals and had become
absorbed by their frenzied activity. He looked up
when Feldman called his name. "Huh? Oh, no,
thanks," he answered with a start. Then looking
back at the tank and smiling: "Cute little fellas."

"They belong in the basement," Feldman said,
"but my wife insists they be allowed to stay here.
They're the only things in the world the child isn't
allergic to. For some reason." Feldman lifted a
crystal whiskey decanter off a shelf and poured
into two old-fashioned glasses. He left them, apparently waiting for ice, and clicked the top
back into the decanter. Then, turning to Schamper: "Lieutenant, I don't want your help."

"I'm not altogether surprised that you say that,
Mr. Feldman. Many parents of kidnapped children react that way because they fear for the lives
of the children. But there's a great deal we can
do—"

"Have you handled a lot of kidnap cases, Lieutenant?"

"No."

"Have you handled *any* other kidnap cases, Lieutenant?"

"Well . . . one, but it was quite different from this."

"How was it different, Lieutenant?"

"A man tried to take his own child away from his divorced wife."

"Then with your limited experience, why do you speak so wisely about how most parents react?"

"It's right out of the training manual at the police academy. . . . Right, Bob?" he added in a lighter tone to the other policeman.

Peseta, startled by the unexpected question, nodded. "Pretty routine, in fact."

The Negro maid came in with a tray of ice and dumped it into an ornate ice bucket. She looked around at all the men in the room, searching their faces for something, and then left.

Feldman took tongs and put two ice cubes into each of the two glasses on the bar counter. He picked up a seltzer bottle and squirted an ounce or so of carbonated water into each glass. He handed a glass to Fred and took a sip from the other. "In spite of your academy training, Lieutenant, and your experience in kidnap cases, and although I'm a textbook parent, I would still prefer to decline your assistance in handling this matter."

"We appreciate your point of view, Mr. Feldman, but we have no intention of withdrawing from the case. Furthermore, the FBI will enter the case very shortly. They officially enter after twenty-four hours, but actually they'll come in as soon as they hear from us. We will do nothing on the outside without first discussing it with you. We appreciate your concern for the child's welfare, and we will see to it there is no press coverage, something, incidentally, you might not be able to manage without our help, if word should leak out. There will be no outward sign of police activity, and no risks will be taken. There will be no police band transmission the kidnappers might pick up. There's a great deal we can do without ever rippling the surface, Mr. Feldman."

"I'm to remain fully in charge and make all decisions," Feldman said.

"We will discuss everything with you."

Feldman paused. "According to the chapter on kidnapping in your academy textbook, what is the first thing we should do?"

"I'd like to question the person who received the contact from the kidnappers. I gather it was one of your maids."

Feldman turned and shouted, *"Sara!"*

She reappeared and looked around apprehensively.

"The lieutenant would like to ask you a few questions, Sara." He touched her arm to assure her. She looked at his hand and then at him. He had never touched her before.

"Sara," said the lieutenant. "When did you notice the child was missing?"

"I looked for him after the man call."

"Then you don't know when or how he was taken?"

"Not till the man call."

"Sara. About what time did you receive the call?"

"'Bout six."

Schamper took a small leather loose-leaf notebook from his inside jacket pocket and began jotting notes. "Sara, tell me everything he said and everything you said as nearly as you can remember it."

"He ask for Mr. Feldman. I say he not here. He ask for Mrs. Feldman. I say she not here. He say Mr. Feldman better get home if he ever want to see Gary alive. I say Gary right here. He say he got Gary. He say he call back tomorrow. Then he hang up."

"Did he say anything else you can remember?"

She wrinkled her moon face as she concentrated, whispering to herself as part of her process of recall. Then she looked at the lieutenant with guilt that bordered on caricature.

"What else did he say?" the lieutenant asked quietly.

"He say no police."

Schamper smiled to give her confidence. "They all say that, Sara. Can you think of anything else he said?"

"That's all."

"What did he sound like? Any—well, any accent? Would you know his voice if you heard it again."

"He just a man. . . . He sound mean."

"What time would you guess Gary was taken? When did you see Gary last before the call?"

She went into her process of recall again. "'Bout three."

"Then he was taken between three and six. Was he outside or in the house?"

"Gary never go outside to play," she said.

"He stays in most of the time," Feldman said. "He's not a very robust child. A respiratory problem. The house is air-conditioned."

"Who was here when it happened, Sara?"

"Jus' me and Janeeta."

"Did Janeeta see anything or notice anything at all?"

"She as surprised as me when I told her about the call."

"OK, Sara. Thanks. That's all for now. If I have any more questions, I'll come see you in the kitchen."

"You think we gonna get the child back all right?"

"Sure. I think so."

She choked up. "We oughta keep the door locked."

"You're right about that," the lieutenant said as she walked out. "Apparently, they just walked in here between three and about five, picked up the child and walked back out," he said to Feldman. "You say there's no chance the child wandered out?"

"The child's allergic to damn near everything. The air in here is carefully filtered. He stays right here. Rather than send him to school, we have him tutored here. He seldom goes outside the house, and then only in my car. Sara was probably in the kitchen and Janeeta upstairs. That's where they usually are."

"I want some pictures of the boy, and tell me everything you can think of about him and anything else that comes to mind that might have the slightest bearing. We'll come out and put some electronic devices on the phone, and we'll be here at all times, but in plain clothes and plain cars, in fact, completely out of sight unless this is impossible."

Feldman handed the lieutenant an eight-by-ten color portrait of the child off a shelf in the room. "His hair is just that red. . . . Apparently they didn't know Isobel was away since they asked for both of us."

"I doubt that—the way they obviously knew their way around."

Feldman lifted his brows—a sign of appreciation for the lieutenant's last comment. "Lieutenant, you handle this case to my satisfaction, and there's a little something in it for you."

Schamper studied Feldman. "I only hope we're successful in getting the child back safely."

Fred put his glass down very quietly. "Victor, I think I'll run ahead home now. I'll see you tomorrow as we discussed." Then, glancing at Schamper and back at Feldman, he added, "I'm not worried."

9

"How about a little blackjack, partner?" Harry had returned from feeding the child.

Roy was sprawled on a sofa in front of the TV. "What for? You got some money you wanna give me? Wait till after payday and I'll take your half away from you."

Harry leaned against the kitchen counter and examined the deck of cards. He broke open the box and slid the cards out. "We got a lotta sitting around to do. It'll kill a little time." He sat down at the end of the table and began shuffling the cards.

Roy got up and came into the kitchen. He took a bottle of beer out of the refrigerator and twisted the cap off. After taking a couple of swallows, he put it down on the table. He picked up the whiskey and a glass off the counter and dumped in a couple of ounces. Then, filling the rest of the glass with beer, he took a large swallow and drained the bottle into the glass. "Harry, the more I sit and think about this thing, the more it comes up we gotta get rid of the kid. I can't see any other way." He spoke in a slow, quiet and persuasive tone.

"How about handing me a beer? How about a little cards?"

"*You* play cards." Roy opened the refrigerator and took out a bottle of beer.

"Let's stick to the book." Harry wiped his hand on his pants and then twisted the bottle cap off, tossing it at the sink. "The kid's never seen us, and he don't know where he is. He'll still be that way when we dump him, still alive and blind-folded."

"Too many things can go wrong when we go to leave him somewhere to be found. Our chances are a lot better if we put him under a shrub in the yard or drop him in the sound," Roy continued in his cool, quiet manner.

"We get the money and give the kid back and they won't chase us long. We kill the kid and they'll never stop chasing us."

"Without the kid they got nothing to go on."

"We go by the book. We don't have to kill the kid. I'll throw a scare into him and he'll never tell nobody nothing."

"Harry." The restraint was suddenly gone from his voice. "I may have to do a little changing on your book. I may have to add a chapter or two, and the new chapter just might be about you if you try and stick my neck in a noose."

"There's no use talking about it now. Let's get our hands on the money first."

"It may not pay to wait that long."

"We need the kid on the phone. Once they hear him, they'll deliver."

Roy drained his drink, made another boilermaker and, without commenting further to Harry, went back to the sofa in front of the TV.

Harry rubbed himself on the neck briefly and then wiped his face on his shirt shoulder. He took a sip of beer. He threw the cards aside and pulled a worn penknife from his pocket. Then he produced a small wood block from a pocket. It was grainless hardwood, around two inches long and an inch square. After studying the block from all angles, he began to chip at it ineffectually with the small pointed blade of the knife.

In the bedroom the child lay on his back, his shackled feet close to the posts at the foot of the bed. Images proliferated, sparkled and oozed on the screens of his closed eyes as he listened to the sounds of the house—the creaks of the sofa; the steady low garble of the TV; the occasional scrape of the chair on the kitchen floor; the occasional thunk of the refrigerator door. He had listened to the quiet conversation in the kitchen but had not made much of it out, picking up only snatches of it over the TV, a word here and there, hardly enough to make sense from it. He had been able to make out more of the louder, in fact, half-shouted exchanges in the hall earlier. He wondered about some of the fragments he had been able to understand. The names, for instance. He felt as if Harry must have known him before. He was totally fearful of Roy.

He picked at the corners of the tape below

his ears, pulling lightly at them, peeling them very, very slowly. They were stuck tight. He peeled, and with every shifting sound in the house, smoothed the peeled ends lightly back down. It became a game: peel, smooth, peel farther, smooth.

The evening dragged on. Roy spent it between the sofa and the refrigerator. Harry spent it grubbing at the wood block with the small bone-handled knife. A dozen empties stood on the table, the counter and in the bag on the floor.

At eleven o'clock Harry walked into the living room. Roy was asleep on the sofa. Harry dropped himself into a chair and watched the news until eleven thirty. No mention of the kidnapping. He hadn't expected any.

The child smoothed the tape down as he heard Harry's footsteps in the hall. He had peeled the two cross strips up onto his cheeks, almost to the point where they crossed the original strip around his head. He sat up in bed as Harry walked into the room. Hearing Harry flip on the overhead light, the child said, "I have to go to the bathroom again."

Harry was startled slightly by the child sitting upright and talking as the light went on. "Oh. Sure, kid." Sitting on the edge of the bed, he drew the string and key from his pocket and unlocked one side of the handcuffs. He led the child to the bathroom and back and reshackled him.

"I usually have something to drink before bed. Milk." The child said it in a withdrawn manner. He had asked to go to the bathroom. Asking for two things might be overtaxing their hospitality. But in his eight years he had become condition-reflexed to have milk at bedtime.

"Sure, kid." Harry left and returned with a small glass, two-thirds filled. He eased it up to meet the child's lips. The child touched Harry's fingers as he brought his own hands up to hold the glass. Harry listened and smiled at the little tick of each swallow. When the child stopped drinking and pulled his hands away, Harry eased the glass down. He again took his left hand and grabbed the neck of the child's shirt and pulled it up to wipe the child's mouth.

"What are you men going to do with me?"

"Nothing, if you do everything we tell you. And you'll do it if you know what's good for you." He spoke sternly. It was time to get back to work.

"But I don't understand." The child hesitated. "Are you going to take me back home?"

"We're going to send you back home if you do everything we tell you to do, exactly how we tell you."

"What do I have to do?"

"Just do everything we tell you. Or we might not be so nice to you. And another thing. After you get home, don't tell nobody nothing about where you've been or who you were with. Is that clear? Don't tell nobody nothing. . . . Don't even tell them why you're not telling them anything. Is that clear? If you do, we're gonna come and get you again and take you away."

"Take me where?"

The child's response confused Harry. The child

sounded almost excited. "Somewhere you won't like going. Understand? Somewhere you won't like going at all."

"I know, but where? It might not be so bad if I didn't have my eyes all taped."

"You touch that tape and I'll shave your head and tape it so it'll never come off. That clear?"

"Where will you take me if I tell about where I've been?"

"Someplace you won't come back from."

"You mean you would kill me?"

"Just don't talk about where you've been."

"How will you know if I've told anyone? You'll have no way of knowing."

"We'll know. You understand? We'll know. And we'll come and get you and take you someplace you won't like so well."

"But how will you know? Who's going to tell you? Sara?"

"Maybe."

"Or Janeeta?"

"Maybe."

"Or maybe Mr. Goldschmidt?"

"Maybe— Who's he?"

"He's my tutor. He comes to our house to teach me."

"Teach you what?"

"Everything . . . except piano."

"Who teaches you piano?" Harry was smiling.

"Old Mrs. Lurgin. She only comes once a week, thank goodness."

"Why thank goodness?"

"Because she doesn't smell much like a flower."

"Don't you go to school at all, Redhead? Do you just stay home all the time?"

The child grew quieter. "My mother wants me to stay home because of all my allergies. She let Mr. Goldschmidt take me a few places like to the Bronx Zoo and a museum and two movies, *Mary Poppins* and *The Sound of Music*."

"Don't your parents ever take you anywhere?"

"I remember going once with them to see my grandparents, but I got sick and started wheezing, so I see my grandparents mostly when they come to our house."

"Did you get sick when you went out with Mr. Goldschmidt?"

"No. That was fun."

"Frankly, Redhead, I think—" Harry stopped. He got up from his sitting position on the child's bed and walked around the bed to the other twin bed and sat down. "I think it's time we both go to sleep. And remember everything I told you tonight. If we let you go back home and you tell anybody anything, we'll come and get you again."

"I wouldn't mind if you came and got me." The child was speaking slowly in a tiny voice. "If we could go somewhere besides here and I didn't have to have this tape on my eyes." He began to choke up. "But I wouldn't like it if"—he stopped himself—"if . . . that other man in there came and got me. I don't like that other man. I hope the police get him."

"Well, he's the one who'll come and get you if you don't do everything I tell you."

"Well, I don't like him," the child said in his

tiniest voice. "I don't like him at all." He shuddered slightly, and a wheeze in his breathing began to become audible. He reached into his pocket and pulled out the nebulizer and began twisting and adjusting. He stuck the long neck in his mouth and inhaled once, then again. He shook it and tried again. "I think I'm out of medicine."

"You'll have to make it without it for a while. You probably need a doctor's prescription to get any of that stuff."

"I don't suppose you could call Dr. Berman."

"I don't think so." Harry had his shoes off.

"There's a kind that works pretty well that you can get without a prescription."

"We'll get you some of that kind in the morning." Harry dropped back onto the pillow. He straightened and flexed his knees a time or two. "Go to sleep."

The child dropped back on the bed and turned on his side and became quiet. Harry lay and watched his tiny silent form. Why, hell, the little kid was practically crying out for company! Just company. Any kind of company. Just something to do. Anything. All that money, too. Harry closed his eyes and turned on his side.

When Harry's breathing became noisy and regular, the child sat up in bed. He sat motionless for several minutes and just listened to Harry's snoring. Then he began peeling on the bottoms of the tape strips with both hands. Within minutes he had the crossed strips up to the strip around his head. Pulling slowly at it, he soon had his eyes uncovered. He continued working at it until he finally pulled the tape free from his head. He dropped it on the bed and sat and studied Harry in the dim light that leaked in from the hall. Then, reaching down, he slipped off his shoes and tried squeezing his feet through the handcuffs. After several futile attempts, he pushed his socks down through the cuffs and off his feet. He began working his bare feet against the steel and, by turning at an odd angle and pointing his toes, forced one cuff off. He whimpered softly because it hurt. Then he worked the other foot free.

Sitting for another moment, he watched Harry, who snorted and shifted position slightly, one arm flopping down. Then he slipped his socks back on and climbed off the bed. Tiptoeing to the window, he parted the curtains and put his hands up to the glass to look out. He couldn't even make out the ground in the inky darkness outside. Moving soundlessly down the hall toward the front of the house, he stood and studied Roy's flickering silvery-white form slumped on the sofa in front of the television. The sofa was next to the front door.

The child turned and padded into the kitchen and to the back door. He began trying the door, looking back over his shoulder at the doorway to the living room. He twisted and pulled at the knob but couldn't open it. He stopped, turned and squatted down onto his haunches with his back against the door. He sat for several minutes, listening to nothing, staring at the living-room wall and the vague, dancing light patterns. Then, standing up, he tried the door again. He found the knob to the deadlatch and turned it. The door opened easily.

He stepped out onto the stoop. It was a dark, overcast night. He could see nothing but blackness —thick, total blackness. He could not even distinguish the trees rustling only a few yards away. He couldn't see any lights in any direction from the stoop. Suddenly, a dog barked viciously not too far away. "No, no, please," the child gasped, almost choked with the remembrance of some past terror. He stepped quickly back up into the doorway. It was very, very dark. And where could he possibly go? At home he slept with a small light burning in his room.

Closing the door and turning the deadlatch, he padded silently back down the hall without glancing again at Roy. He went back into the bedroom, leaving the door wide open to get as much light as possible from the small hall light. Walking over to Harry's bed, he stood and watched Harry sleep for several minutes. Then he climbed back onto his own bed.

Slipping off his socks, he worked his bare feet back into the handcuffs. He pulled on his socks, slipping them up through the cuffs, and then put on his shoes. He picked up the tape, which had gotten stuck to itself in two places, and peeled it open. He carefully put it back into place on his face and around his head and tamped it out smooth. Dropping back onto the bed, he turned on his side and went to sleep.

10

Harry was lying in tall grass. He was in an open
field, the ground around him wet and muddy, the
tall grass growing up out of the mud in thin
straight strands. Trying to focus on the linear,
thatched pattern, he stared off through the stand
of grass surrounding him in all directions. What
time of day was it? Just before dawn? So little
light. Was he in the New Jersey meadows? Perhaps he was in the meadows. Secaucus. He must
be in Secaucus. There were pigs around. Were
there still pigs in Secaucus? Must be. He could
sense their presence. He could hear them. One of
them touched him! Yeah! It nudged at his side
and then bounded away when he slapped at its
snout. Playful little fella, the way it jumped and
scooted away from the slap across its nose! He
didn't even bother to turn over and look at the
little fella. He waited and heard the little fella
walk slowly back up and root at his side again. He
flung a limp hand at the little animal, and again

it scampered back, moving without uttering a sound.

"Hogs won't bother you none if you're movin'," Tex Forney used to tell him in the Army. Tex was from somewhere in rural Kentucky, and Harry was from the city. "They won't bother you none as long as you're movin'. But they'll eat anythin', dead or alive, if they can get it between their jaws. Provided it don't fight back much. Why, hell, hogs'll eat a man if he's out cold in the middle of their pasture. They'll walk up to him and smell of him and if he don't do nothin', they'll root at him a time or two, and if he still don't do nothin', why, hell, they might just bite at him. And if he still don't do nothin', they might just eat him up. They look like nothin', but sometimes I think they're pretty smart. I think they can tell when somethin's in trouble. I think they can smell fear. And they'll take advantage. I remember I had a dog loved to chase the hogs and get 'em to runnin'. One day they accidently ran over the dog tryin' to get away from him and they messed him up pretty good. They stopped runnin' and turned around and came walkin' back, sniffin' and root'n, and when they saw that dog was in trouble, they ate him. I didn't actually see 'em eat 'im, but the dog disappeared and never came back and a while after that I saw some fur that looked like his out there where the hogs were and half a dozen times I saw him almost get run over when he got to chasin' 'em. Musta been what happened. Hell, they'll eat anythin'. They'll eat a man."

Harry felt the pig nuzzle him in the side again.

He shouldn't be lying there so lifelessly with those pigs all around him. "I had one hog weighed close to fifteen hundred pounds when I finally sold him. Why, hell, I'll bet that sucker could eat a man by himself. Had jaws on him could take a man's thigh. . . ." Harry felt a sick fear engulf him. The pig rooted at his side again, and he moved away from it, inchworming along the ground. His body felt leaden and disabled. He tensed up, waiting for the next touch of the pig's snout, and when it came, burrowing into his hip, he grabbed it and held it and looked at it in the dim light and looked up. "Wha'?" The pig's snout was Roy's hand. Harry sat bolt upright in the bed.

"Gimme the key to the cuffs."

"What?"

"Gimme the key to the cuffs."

Harry snorted and rubbed his face with both hands. Then he glanced over at the motionless child in the other bed with the cross-taped face.

"What've you done?"

"Nothin', yet. Gimme the key."

Harry climbed out of bed and walked around the other bed and out into the hall. He went into the bathroom and relieved himself, frowning at the glare-white brilliance of the enameled room flooded by light. He walked back out into the semidark hall to Roy. He was more nearly awake. "What time is it?"

"Three."

"What are you doing up?"

"Gimme the key."

"What for?"

"What do you think for?"

"Goddammit, Roy, we'll never get the money without the kid!"

"You're crazy, Harry. . . . I should have throttled the little bastard and then got the key. That's what I get for trying to be neat."

"Roy, don't be a goddamn idiot!"

They stared at each other for a prolonged moment, and then Harry walked back to the bedroom, leaving Roy standing. Harry sat on the edge of his bed and checked his pocket for the key. He took it out and transferred it to his other pocket. Then he stood up and climbed into bed with the child, turning on his side with the child in front of him. The key was in the pocket under him. The child took a deep breath and then changed his position slightly, smacking his lips in his sleep.

11

Victor Feldman reached over from the high canopied bed and picked up the phone after the first ring. He was a light sleeper, and this tendency was almost a facet of his business philosophy; alertness and mental agility at all times are prerequisites for winners. One must be able to come out of sleep into the middle of a negotation if necessary, an old one or a new one, and know where he is and how his next move must be played and exactly how hard, buying *or* selling, he can push. One must be able, at any moment, to seize control of the interaction and drag it to the precipitous edge, indeed, hold it out over the edge, and know just when to pull back, having gotten all there is to be gotten without losing control. And if one must wake up out of sleep into this situation, he must instinctively have full faculties, instantaneous full power. Winners cannot tolerate a condition of stupor. Leave stupors to the stupid.

"Hello?" He heard the click of another extension being lifted somewhere else in the house.

"Victor."

"Barney, what could you possibly want at this hour?" He was fully awake.

"Victor, do you mean you were asleep? Really, Victor. My God. Even I haven't been able to sleep thinking about Gary."

"Barney, what do you want?"

"Have you heard anything from the kidnappers?"

"Nothing." Feldman sat up, turned and rested his feet on the side of the high bed.

"Nothing at all?"

"Is that what you called for? Barney, how often do you plan to call to check up on things?"

"My God, Victor, you don't even sound concerned."

"Goddammit, Barney, of course I'm concerned."

"What are the police doing?"

"Whatever it is that police do. They're doing their job." He paused. "They're investigating."

"Are they there now?"

"Yes. They stayed over." He resisted the urge to disclose that they were listening on a downstairs extension.

"Victor, is there anything I can do?"

"If what you've already done is a sample of what you'd like to do for me, do me a favor and resist the urge to do me any further good turns."

There was a pause. Friedlander finally spoke in a very subdued tone. "What was that supposed to mean?"

"You know damn well what."

"Victor?" His voice was injured, confused.

"Why did you call the police in on this thing?" Feldman snarled. "You've placed Gary's life in jeopardy."

"Gary's . . . life? . . . What? Victor, when a child has been kidnapped you call the police. What is this? I did what I know was the right thing to do. What would you have done, Victor? What would you have done? You'd have done the same thing. The exact same thing. I can't understand for the life of me your attitude."

"Are you quite finished?"

"Quite."

"I gave Isobel specific instructions to tell everyone there not to call back here and not to spread the word and not to call the police—"

"I never got that message."

Feldman remained quiet for a moment. "Barney, how many people did you call besides the police?"

"You underestimate me, Victor. You see? I think more like you than you give me credit for. I called no one else."

"We don't want the story to break."

"Of course not. Victor, anything I can do?"

"Would you like to put up some money?"

"If you needed money, I'd be the first to try and help out. But face it, Victor, one thing you have is money. You're a natural target."

"If I needed money, they wouldn't have taken Gary. One thing is abundantly clear. Whoever they are, they have good information."

"So what's next?"

"We're waiting to hear from them."

"Let me know if I can do anything for you."

"We'd better clear the line. We don't know when they'll try to call."

"Things'll work out, Victor. There's no money in hurting Gary."

"Thanks, Barney. You're a great comfort. We'd better hang up." Feldman hung up. He eased off the bed, went into the carpeted bathroom, returned to the bed and sat again on the edge, his feet on the massive wood plank running alongside the mattress. He picked up the phone again and dialed. "Uh, Lieutenant, uh, if you don't mind—" He heard a click.

A sleepy woman's voice answered. "Hello?"

"No problems getting home last night, I gather." His voice was soft and warm, almost tender.

"Oh!" A pause. "Oh, Victor." Another pause as she struggled to focus. "Oh, no, of course not. Victor, have you heard anything from the kidnappers? From Gary?"

"Nothing yet."

"They won't harm Gary. I feel sure they won't."

"Whoever they are, I'm sure they must realize that it would be anything but sound business. They'd be sacrificing all their bargaining power." His tone was venomous.

"Oh, Victor. I'm sure everything will be all right."

"I would like having you with me this morning," he said, the warmth flooding back into his voice. "I need you now, even though—"

"Yes, I know." She said it quickly, to interrupt him, as though he were about to say something

76

she had heard many times before and always found distasteful.

"That's just how I am. Different men have different needs."

"Yes, I know." She sounded patient.

"But I suppose it's out of the question for the moment. I've got to stay here by the phone. They're supposed to call me today. Unfortunately, I don't see how we can arrange it."

"I'm sure it would be better."

"At least till they've made contact and I know what they expect me to do. Then perhaps I can come to your place."

"When do you expect your wife back?"

"Who knows?" His tone was sarcastic, almost a bitter laugh. "She'll probably show up some time late today or tomorrow. But so what?"

She remained quiet for a moment. "It's almost time for me to leave for work."

"Yes, of course," he said with a sudden abruptness.

"Please keep me informed about Gary."

"Rest assured."

"I guess we'd better get off the phone."

"I'll speak to you later." He hung up. He slipped out of his pajamas, walked into the bathroom and turned on the shower.

12

Harry made coffee. He put two mugs and a package of A&P doughnuts on the table. Roy walked into the kitchen wearing the jacket he had worn the day before. And he had shaved. But his eyes were vividly red-rimmed from the boilermakers, and his face was drawstrung from a brutal headache.

"Well, don't you look nice!" Harry said.

"I need the coat."

"You need something besides a coat," Harry said, still trying to be funny. "What do you need with a coat?" he asked after thinking a moment. The day already felt warm.

"I need it," Roy piped.

"You gotta get the kid some medicine."

"You mentioned it."

"You don't need a coat for that."

"Maybe I do. Slobs wouldn't be buying that kind of medicine. Anyhow, I like using the coat pocket for the glasses."

"You're not planning to go anywhere besides for the medicine?"

"Now where else would I be going?" Roy snapped.

Harry laughed. "I can't imagine. When you go, don't forget to go at least to Stratford before trying a drugstore. The cops may have done a little calling around." He took the coffeepot and began pouring it.

Roy broke his way into the package of doughnuts. "What's the name of the medicine we need for our patient?"

"We'll have to ask him again. That's not the kind of thing I make a habit of knowing about."

Roy dunked a doughnut and sloshed the dripping section into his mouth. "Jesus," he said, his face dribbling food, "I never thought I'd be playing doctor with the kid."

"We'll be talking money with his old man this afternoon," Harry said. "Think about that instead."

The change of subject seemed to satisfy Roy, who ate four doughnuts and drained the mug of coffee without commenting further. Harry also ate without speaking again.

They finished and walked into the bedroom, where the child was lying on his side, his legs twisted to accommodate the steel handcuffs. His body seemed relaxed, but there was no way to tell if he was asleep or awake because so much of his face was covered by tape. Harry sat on the edge of the bed and put a hand on the child's shoulder. "Hey, Redhead."

The child rolled over on his back. There was still no way of knowing if he had been asleep.

"Hey, Redhead," Harry repeated with a firmer grip and shake of the child's shoulder.

The child pushed himself into an upright position.

"Redhead, what's the name of the medicine we have to get for you?"

"Is the other man here?"

"He's here. He's going out to get the medicine."

The child reached in his pocket and pulled out the nebulizer. "You take this in and they can call Dr. Berman and he'll tell them how to refill it."

"We can't do that. You told me last night there's a kind you get without a prescription that works almost as well."

"This kind works better."

"You'll have to settle for the other kind. What's the name of the other kind?"

"I'd be better off with this kind," the child said in his characteristic tiny voice.

"What's the name of the other kind, Redhead? Quick, now."

The child remained quiet for a moment. "It's called Asma-neft Solution A-four." He said it with complete businesslike certainty.

"Wait a minute," Harry said. He turned to Roy. "You better write it down."

Roy walked over to the desk and began impatiently shuffling through the contents of the middle drawer. He slammed the drawer shut and walked out of the room. Harry sat and watched him.

While waiting, he dried his upper lip on the shoulder of his shirt and then treated himself to a hand on the back of the neck. He rubbed long and hard. Finally, he dropped his hands, resting his elbows on his knees, and waited. The child lay quiet. The sound of Roy rummaging in the kitchen, drawers opening and closing and cabinet doors slamming, suddenly stopped and Roy reappeared with the yellow stump of a pencil and a scrap of brown kraft paper from a grocery bag.

"What was that name again?" Roy asked.

"What was it again?" Harry asked the boy.

"Asma-neft Solution A-four," the child repeated.

Roy stood at the desk and wrote, the pencil and paper at arm's length.

"I hope you don't plan to pull that out in the store," Harry said.

Roy flipped the pencil at the desk and ignored it when it went over the back of the desk onto the floor. Without looking back at Harry or the boy, he walked out of the room.

Harry sat without moving while listening to Roy's steps down the hall, down the steps, into the car. He waited for the car door to slam and the motor to turn over. He followed the car's progress out of the garage, out the driveway and down the street. He stared at the fragile faceless child, lying back once again on the bed, his torso filling and shrinking with each just-audible breath.

He reached out and gave the kid's shoulder a reassuring squeeze. "So what d'ya say, Redhead?"

"Good morning." The child shrugged.

Harry smiled. "What else do you say?"

"I guess it must be morning. It's still night under this stupid tape."

"It's morning," Harry said. "Good morning to *you*."

"Wonder how my gerbils are?" the boy said, somewhat reflectively.

"Which?"

"I have gerbils."

"That what you take the medicine for?"

"Gerbils. Gerbils. They're little pets. They're called pocket kangaroos."

"Pocket kangaroos." Harry nodded his head. "Say, do you have to take a leak?"

The child hesitated. Unfamiliar terminology. "I guess a little."

"Might as well, then," Harry said. "It'll save going later."

"Might as well," the child said.

Harry fished in his pocket and pulled out the small key with the little bit of string on it. The key reminded him of Secaucus and pigs, making him shudder. He unlocked the handcuffs and slipped them off the sticklike ankles. Then he guided the boy off the bed. He was becoming adept at leading the blindfolded child with one firm hand around his arm. He could change direction with the slightest twist or move him forward or slow him up. And the child walked almost assured, his arms not outstretched, but more or less down. Harry thought of the frail arms as pretzel sticks— too rough a grip and SNAP!

Leading the child back to the bed, he snapped the handcuffs back in place. "I'd offer to have you wash your teeth, Redhead, but we don't have your toothbrush here."

"I don't wash them every day at home either."

"Why not?" Harry asked, smiling.

"Just works out that way."

"You say it just works out that way?"

"I like to wait till after breakfast so the toothpaste taste doesn't spoil the taste of my orange juice and so I usually wait till after breakfast to wash them and sometimes I never quite seem to make it back upstairs to wash them." The child was smiling, obviously delighted to be able to confide this little bit of daring.

"What does your mother say?"

"She's either asleep or not at home."

"What about your father?"

"He's usually not at home either. He usually has other things on his mind anyway."

"What about all of those maids you've got in that house? What do they say?"

"Sara tells me to go wash my teeth after breakfast."

"What do you say to her?" Harry was grinning.

"I tell her to go wash *her* teeth."

"And what does she say to that?"

The child was smiling. "She says I'm not much good and that I remind her of someone she knows. Besides, I don't wash them on purpose when Mrs. Lurgin comes."

"Who's Mrs.—whatever you said?"

"I told you last night. Weren't you listening?"

"I was listening. I forgot. She the one that smells?"

"You can believe it."

"Fight fire with fire, huh, Redhead? Speaking of breakfast, how about a little?"

The child shrugged. " I suppose so."

"I'd ask you what you'd like, only we haven't got that much selection."

"What do you have?"

"How's doughnuts and milk?"

"What about orange juice and cereal?"

"We ain't got orange juice. Fresh out."

"Well, could I have cereal and milk?"

"What's wrong with doughnuts? I thought kids went for doughnuts."

"They might have eggs in them."

"Eggs in doughnuts? Why, hell, even if it said eggs on the package, why, there's not enough eggs in those doughnuts—"

"I can't eat any poultry products."

"I know. You told me."

"You could check the list of ingredients on the package. Or else you could let me have cereal and milk."

"Cereal and milk's too much trouble. By the time I finish feeding you a bowl of that, even if I can find any, you and this bed'd be a mess."

"You could take the tape off my eyes and let me feed myself."

"The tape stays put," Harry said firmly.

"I don't know why. I already know what you look like."

The easy look left Harry's face. "What are you talking about?"

The child sensed the change in Harry's tone. He thought about the afternoon before when Roy had come into the house and grabbed him and carried him out to the truck. He brought back and concentrated on the glimpse he had gotten of the man driving, the heavyset man with the graying hair and the funny mustache and the friendly face. He recalled studying him the night before in the bedroom in the dim light. The mustache had been gone. Roy's mustache had also been gone when he saw him sitting in the living room asleep. He would be expected to have seen the two men on the day they came to pick him up. "I saw you yesterday," the child said. "You can't keep from seeing someone if you happen to look at them."

"If somebody asked you what I look like, what would you say? How would you say I look?"

"You have a mustache."

"Anything else?"

"You have gray hair, and"—the child shrugged —"you're about my daddy's size, I'd guess."

"Anything else?"

"The mustache could have been a fake."

Harry grabbed the child by the arm. "Why do you say that?"

"Well, it could have been. And Roy's could have been, too."

Harry grabbed the child roughly by the shoulders, a tiny shoulder in each of his large lumpy mechanic's hands. *"What did you say?"*

"About what?" The child cowered in Harry's abrupt, wrenching grasp.

"About the other man?"

The child knew he had made a bad mistake. The little bit of his face showing beneath the tape began to screw up. "I just said your mustaches that I saw you with when you came to get me could have been fakes. I didn't say they were. I just said they could have been."

"Besides that," Harry snapped. "What did you call the other man?"

The child's mouth twisted up and he sniffled. "You can't keep from hearing something if you hear it. You can't just say I didn't hear what I just heard."

Harry gripped the child tighter. "What did you say you heard the other man's name was?"

"I thought I heard you call him Roy yesterday."

Harry relaxed his grip and then released the boy altogether. He just sat and stared at the boy for several moments. He wiped the lower part of his face and then his brow on the shoulder of his shirt. Then he took the child's shoulders in his hands again, but in a soft, assuring way. "Redhead? Tell me." Harry mustered total restraint. "Did you hear the other man call me by any name?"

The child hesitated. "No, I don't think so."

"Are you sure?" he asked gently. "You know, you just said you can't keep from hearing something if you hear it. It's not your fault if you hear something. Tell me. Did you hear him call me by any name?" He slid his hand down the back of the child's head and neck as he asked. He did it in a comforting, assuring way, like petting a dog.

"What will you do if I say yes?"

"Nothing, Redhead. I told you it wouldn't be your fault."

"Well—" The child hesitated.

"Go ahead, Redhead. Tell me. I told you it's OK."

"Well, once I heard him call you Harry and once I heard him call you Banner, so I guess your name is Harry Banner."

"*No, Redhead!*" Harry's entire body trembled. He let go of the boy and stood up.

"But you told me to. You said it was OK."

Harry stared at the small form sitting on the bed. The oblong, taped-up egg of a head with brilliantly red hair. Perched atop the slender, vulnerable neck. A tiny bundle of vital cords ensheathed in a thin layer of a child's skin. He thought of chickens he had killed when he was young. Take a chicken's head in your hand, a couple of quick, hard shakes, and a headless body is flopping around on the ground, pumping blood from the neck stump. At a younger age he had learned a different, maybe even better technique. Put the chicken on the ground, lay a stick over its head, put your feet on the stick on each side of the chicken's head, grab the chicken's legs, and, with an easy pull, separate the body from the head.

Harry walked away from the boy and began pacing around the room. "Gotta think, gotta think." He began stroking himself on the back of the neck, repeated, vigorous strokes. "Jesus! Jesus!

Jesus! Jesus! Jesus!" He continued pacing, his head bowed, his right hand rubbing his neck.

The child listened to him move from place to place in the room, mumbling, his steps heavy and irregular, with pauses to change direction. "Mr. Banner?" the child called out.

Harry continued pacing.

The child wondered if he should have disobeyed about repeating the name he had learned. But he had been told to say it, encouraged to say it. Then why was Mr. Banner acting so strangely? "Mr. Banner?" he called again. Mr. Banner didn't answer. There was something almost funny about the way Mr. Banner moved about the room, mumbling "Jesus, Jesus" and "Gotta think" over and over and over. He wondered how long Mr. Banner would keep it up. "Mr. Banner?" he said and began to smile as he listened to Mr. Banner continue to pace and mumble "Jesus" and "Gotta think." He thought about the name Banner and pictured an American flag being beaten back and forth in a strong wind. A Star-Spangled Banner. He almost laughed. Harry the Banner. Harry the flag. Hey, Banner, do you yet wave? "Mr. Banner?" he called out. He received no answer. He heard only the pacing and the mumbling. *"Hey, Banner!"*

Harry stopped and looked at the child. The child was grinning! Grinning a grin that disappeared up under the tape on each side of his face. He walked over and sat down on the bed and grabbed the child's shoulders. "What's so goddamn funny?"

"Hey, Banner, do you yet wave? Over the land of the—"

Harry shook the child, who quickly stopped laughing. "Listen, Redhead. Now, listen. You've got to forget the names you told me you heard. Forget 'em! Understand? The other man cannot find out you know. Understand? It's life or death. You know what that means? Life or death? You've got to be careful. You can't slip up. He cannot find out you know, or you're in trouble. Understand?"

The child got very quiet and began to hiccup, then wheeze, finally cry. "What will he do if he finds out I know?"

"We're not going to find out because he's not going to find out. You're not going to slip up with him around. Is that clear?"

"Okay, but what if I do?"

"Just don't. Forget you know the names. Don't use them again. Is that clear?"

The child began to cry harder. "All right already," he said, shuddering with tears.

"Now stop crying. You'll get your bandage wet."

The child worked at getting himself under control.

"That's better," Harry said. "Now settle down. And remember, just don't use any names."

"Banner?"

"What did I just tell you?"

"I won't use any when he's around."

"Stop using them altogether."

The child took a deep breath and shook as he exhaled. His throat whistled as the air went in and out. "What's going to happen?"

"Nothing," Harry answered.

"Something's got to happen. It's impossible for nothing to happen."

"I don't know yet."

"When will . . . he be back with my medicine?"

"Pretty soon. Any minute now. Try and relax and maybe you won't need it."

The child was quiet as if lost in thought for a moment. "I'm ready for my breakfast now."

13

"Mr. Feldman?"

Feldman was having black coffee at his desk in the library. He looked up at the plainclothes policeman who had arrived with Lieutenant Schamper the previous night. The two of them had spent the night on couches in the den. They were being served breakfast when Feldman came down and went to his desk.

"Mr. Feldman, can you please come to the front door? There's someone at the door and I think Sara needs your help."

"What is it?" Feldman asked. His tone was amiable but controlled, efficient. He had finished the newspaper, which lay, neatly closed, to one side, and his briefcase stood open on the desk, the top almost vertical, and he was studying a file of correspondence in a manila folder. Several other folders, some letter size and some legal size, lay on the desk top.

"Could you come to the front door, Mr. Feldman? Some guy's asking directions. We don't think it would be too wise to show ourselves, so you'd best give Sara a little help."

"Certainly." Feldman couldn't remember the officer's name from the night before. He remembered Schamper's, but not this man's. His face almost greenish from his heavy, unshaven beard and his suit badly rumpled, this man was but an element of the background to what was going on. Feldman walked toward the foyer, followed by the officer, who hung back out of sight. Sara confronted the man in the open door. Schamper stood to one side, well out of the man's line of vision.

"Mr. Feldman," Sara said. "This man looking for Fernhill Drive. I don't know 'xactly how to tell him to get there from here. You better tell him."

Feldman glanced at the slim, seedy-looking man standing at the door with horn rims, a mustache, coat and pants that didn't match and a faded sports shirt. The man radiated a heavy body odor. "Who are you looking for on Fernhill?" Feldman asked. "I've a number of friends on Fernhill."

The man cleared his throat and hesitated at the obviously unexpected question. "I gotta make an estimate on a job over there."

"What sort of estimate?" Feldman asked. "What do you do?"

"Mechanic."

"What sort of mechanic?"

"Auto mechanic," the man answered.

"I thought automobile repairs were usually estimated in the repair shops."

"Not this one. This one won't run. I gotta diagnose it."

"Someone's car on Fernhill?" Feldman asked with an incredulous arch of his brows.

"This one broke down on Fernhill." The man's expression suddenly eased. "This one just broke down over there. It doesn't belong to anyone living there."

This seemed to satisfy Feldman. He stepped out of the door, taking pains to stand clear of the man's pronounced stench. He pointed down the street. "Go back to the end of this street and turn left on that one, which is Hickory Hill. Take your second left, then your first right, and then, after a winding stretch, the next left, which is the beginning of Fernhill. You'll see a sign."

"Thanks," the man said. He studied Feldman momentarily and then looked in the door, scanning the interior. Schamper and Peseta stayed clear of his view. Then he turned, walked back to the old Chevy parked under the breezeway, climbed in and started the motor.

As the car began to move slowly toward the mouth of the long driveway, Schamper stepped forward far enough to get a good view of the back of the car. He pulled his small, black leather notebook from his jacket pocket and made a notation. "You know, Mr. Feldman," he said with his easy smile, "you'd make a crackerjack prosecutor."

"Riffraff!" Feldman snapped, still staring at the end of the driveway where the car had disappeared. "I can't stand the smell of riffraff!" Then he relaxed the disdainful look on his face and glanced at Schamper. "I hope you two slept well last night. You really could have used guest rooms as I suggested."

"We slept very well, thanks," Schamper told him.

"Did you enjoy your breakfast?"

"As a matter of fact"—Schamper smiled—"it was the best breakfast I've had in a while. Wouldn't you say so, Bob?"

"If you wish more coffee or anything, don't be bashful. Perhaps you'd like to clean up. A shave and shower or anything like that. The girls will see that you have everything you need."

Schamper glanced at Peseta, who was looking at him rather hopefully. "Well," he hesitated, "well, maybe a little later in the morning when I get everybody out here that I want. Incidentally, to bring you up to date, I'm in touch with the local FBI office, and some of their people should be out any minute. More men will be out from our headquarters shortly, including our chief. There are a number of things we can set up which won't ripple the surface. And as I mentioned last night, we'll put some electronic stuff on the phone for when they make their next contact."

"How do you estimate our chances, Lieutenant?"

"I'd rather not make guesses about such things, Mr. Feldman. Let's hope for the best."

14

Something of a plan began to take vague shape in Harry's mind. If he was going to keep the kid from ever telling his name, he'd have to do it by reaching the kid, really reaching him. A threat would never work. He'd have to make him worry about what would happen to his old friend Harry Banner. His old friend Harry Banner. This was probably the key. When he became the kid's friend, and he rather had the feeling he already was, he would probably be the first member in the club. Jesus, the kid never went out of the house. He just stayed there, shut in with those two black women, seeing a couple visiting teachers once in a while. And who smelled. Christ, it was enough to give a kid asthma. It was enough to give him something.

One thing was for sure. They couldn't let Roy find out the kid knew their names. Roy wouldn't hesitate a minute. Roy held all the cards. No question about that. There was a noose waiting for them, and as of that minute the only person living who knew which necks belonged in the noose was the kid. So what did that spell out? Get rid of the kid. They couldn't let Roy find out the kid knew. Just pick the kid up for company for a couple days, take a little money off a rich man and send the kid back home. No blood. No fuss. How could they have screwed things up so bad with such a stupid mistake? Everything had worked like a well-tuned engine. Smooth. Not a hitch. Every light on the timer cutting in and out perfect.

He'd have to stay between Roy and the kid every second. Never leave Roy alone with the kid. He'd have to get through to the kid and make him understand he just couldn't slip up. At least not for two more days. Two more days and it's a whole new ball game. Two more days. But how do you impress it on him? Try and fill him with the fear of God? You scare the kid and the kid runs scared. No good. He'll start choking up and not be able to keep nothing straight. Can't reach him with a threat. Threaten the kid and he feels threatened. Won't work.

So how do you reach the kid? If not a threat, what? A promise? . . . A promise. You dangle a carrot. What else? Two days, kid. Two days and we swing. Two days and we go places.

Harry surveyed the block of wood. After hours of pecking and gouging, it still looked pretty much like a block of wood. Precious few shavings so far. Christ, he needed a wrench to make things happen. Something with leverage. Force. Whittling was a gentle game. He'd always wished he could whittle. He'd always envied the old guys who did it and made it look so easy. It ain't easy. If he could whittle, he'd be a different man. Things would be different. Closing the knife, he dropped it into one pocket, the block of wood into the other.

He got up from the kitchen table and walked back into the bedroom. The child was sitting up in bed. The tape strips were peeled up from under his ears and the whole bandage lifted enough to expose his eyes. He was looking at Harry with his large eyes and was grinning as Harry entered the room. Harry covered his upper lip with his arm like a surprised naked girl trying to hide her bosom. "Redhead, goddammit! What did I tell you about that bandage?" The child grinned at him a moment longer and then began rolling the bandage back down and smoothing it back into place.

It struck Harry that the child showed no visible surprise on seeing him without the mustache. When they talked the night before, it had been the one thing about his appearance the child had remembered. But then the child had made the comment about the possibility that it might be fake. Why? Who could say? What difference did it make anyway? The rules of the game had changed. In fact, they were changing, it seemed, every minute. They were changing so fast Harry wished he had a scorecard. "How'd you like to see the Pacific Ocean, Redhead?"

"Huh?"

Harry sat down on the edge of the bed and began rubbing at the tape on the boy's head, trying to seal it more securely. "What did I tell you about this tape, Redhead? Didn't I tell you not to touch it?"

"What did you say about the Pacific Ocean?"

"We're talking about this tape right now. You want me to have to get rough with you." He said it with an air of mock sternness he was sure the child could read.

"What about the Pacific Ocean?"

"I said how would you like to see it?"

"When?"

"We could leave tomorrow. Just you and me."

"I wouldn't see much with this stupid tape over my eyes."

"We'll take that off when we get ready to leave."

The child thought for a minute. "You mean you're not going to take me home?"

"What do you want to go home for? You don't have any fun at home."

"You mean I'll never go back home?"

"Oh, sure you will, later on. But first we'll go to California and see the Pacific Ocean."

"You mean we'll just take a trip?"

"That's what I mean."

"For how long?"

"As long as we like. As long as the flavor lasts. Then you come back home."

The child's mouth fell open as the full impact of Harry's proposal began to reach him. "That would be great!"

"I thought you'd like it."

The child got quiet for a moment. "Are we going to call my parents and tell them?" He asked the question in a soft, probing voice, a voice that reflected long-ingrained total obedience to parental control. But it also reflected the fear that this parental control would unquestionably put a quick end to any plan such as this.

Harry thought a moment. "We'll call them from out there."

The child's exuberance came sweeping back. "This is gonna be great! It's gonna be great!"

"There's something you have to do first, Redhead."

"I'll do it. What?"

Harry took the child by the shoulders again. "Now settle down and listen. Settle down and get serious and listen very carefully." Harry paused and watched the child.

"Well?" the child said.

"Now you've got to do this very carefully. One slip and the whole deal is off. Understand? Off! Until we leave tomorrow, you don't touch that tape again. You don't lay a finger on it. Not a finger. Understand? And you don't call nobody around here by their name. Not me, not the other man, nobody. And you don't let on that we've been talking or planning anything. Nothing. Understand? Like we don't know each other. Not friends— strangers. Understand? Because if the other man picks up a clue, things'll be all queered up. But good. I'm serious, Redhead. This is what you got to do and you can't blow it. Everything's riding on it. Everything. You understand? Everything."

The child didn't speak. He was concentrating on his assignment.

"Just till tomorrow when we get ready to go, Redhead. Till tomorrow when I take that tape off you. Till then you just stay there and do nothing and say nothing."

"What if I need something? Like to go to the bathroom?"

"Ask me like I was a stranger. That's all. Just like you did yesterday."

The child shrugged his shoulders.

"I'm counting on you, Redhead. Win yourself a trip to California. And maybe the great Northwest."

"And Roy's—and the other man's not coming with us?"

"Not if you don't blow it."

"I won't blow it," the child said, once again back in his special tiny voice.

"I'm gonna leave you now. Going back in the other room to wait. You take it easy. OK? Take it easy and think it over."

15

"Guess who I just met?" Roy walked into the kitchen carrying a heavy grocery sack and set it on the counter. He pulled a small white bag out of his jacket pocket and flipped it onto the table where Harry sat whittling.

"Where'd you buy this?" Harry asked, picking up the package.

"Stratford. Didn't you say Stratford? I went to Stratford." Roy lifted two six-packs of beer out of the grocery sack.

"Oh, yeah. It says so right here." Harry studied the pharmacy's advertising on the bag. He pulled the small package out of the bag and began squinting at the medical language.

"Guess who I just met?"

"I can't imagine. The chief of police?"

"Victor Feldman."

"Where? At the drugstore? Buying me a box of cigars, I guess."

"I went by his house."

"What are you, a wise guy?"

"I just wanted to prove to you that we're total strangers to everybody but that kid in there."

Harry looked up in disbelief. "What, are you trying to make some kind of a funny?"

"I'm telling ya I went over there."

"In your own car?"

"Jesus, that Feldman is an ugly bastard. It'll make me feel one hell of a lot better to take a wad off him."

Harry stood up. "Are you serious? You went driving up there in your own car?"

"Not much going on. Nobody around. No cops, nothing."

"*You moron! You moron! You stupid moron!* How stupid do you think those cops are? Of course they were there. You think they're gonna come out and shake hands? Don't you know one phone call and they've got the whole book on you? And me?"

"You're crazy. The last person in the world they're going to check up on is some guy who comes walking up to the door."

"A kid's been snatched out of that house. They're going to check everything. Twice."

"Don't get your ass in an uproar, Harry. They ain't interested in me. Not till that kid in there points the finger at me anyway." But Roy sounded very uncertain.

"You stick my neck in a noose and tell me not to get my ass— What address is on your car registration?"

"Herman Street."

"That the only address you use?"

"The only one."

"Once they get rolling, they'll run this place down. Your name's on a deed somewhere. Time. How much time?" Harry dried his face on his shoulder and began his neck massage. "What'd you tell 'em you were doing there?"

"Told 'em I was looking for Fernhill for a car to give an estimate on." Roy's confidence picked up slightly.

"How'd you manage to do something that smart?" At least the story would fit. At least he didn't spit out some stupid story that wouldn't check out with the plates on the car. He *was* a mechanic. He *did* own a garage. . . . And he had a two-time loser on his payroll! And one who had a sister working for Victor Feldman!

Once again, it was a new ball game. Roy had pulled the stupidest stunt in history. He didn't hold all the cards anymore. Things were different. The case for not hurting the kid was really looking smarter all the time. Yessir. New game. New rules.

And the odds on winning anything were dropping like a rock.

Roy stared at the mutilated little block of wood and the penknife in Harry's hands and snickered. "You still trying to carve on oak? Christ, that wood's harder than steel. You couldn't whittle that wood with a power saw. That little blade? Jesus, trying to whittle oak with that little toothpick is like"—he snickered again—"it's like trying to bang out a busted fender with a loaf of bread." He grinned. He was proud of that comparison. "King whittler, Harry. That's what you are. World's champion whittler. . . . Get a piece of cedar. Or pine. You know how you whittle, Harry? About like you fix cars."

But Harry had paid no attention to Roy's attempted comeback. Harry was weighing options. Resting his right hand on the tabletop, he allowed the penknife to slip down into his fingers. Closing his fist around the handle, he stared at the small blade protruding, erect, menacing. Then he lifted his right arm to wipe his face on his sleeve and went back to whittling.

16

The telephone rang, and Feldman picked it up quickly.

"Hello."

"Victor. I'm at Kennedy."

"Isobel. Oh, it's you. I didn't expect you quite so soon."

"I was able to get out almost immediately. I left everything. The hotel will pack and ship my things. Have you heard from the baby?"

"No."

"Nothing? You haven't heard from the kidnappers at all? Not a thing?"

"No. Listen. I don't want to talk now. I don't want to tie up the phone. We'll talk when you get here."

"Victor, can you come and get me?"

"Have you completely lost your— Isobel. I'm sorry. No. I can't leave here. I'll send a car, but I suspect it would be faster if you used the limousine and let us pick you up here. They leave every hour."

"Victor, please. Those limousines are always very crowded."

"I'll send a car. Which airline?"

"Pan Am. Victor, did you call George Berman?"

"What possibly for?"

"Gary must have his medication."

"What do you expect George to do, make a house call wherever they're holding Gary? If Gary needs medicine, I'm sure he'll tell them about it."

"Victor, please. Call George."

"Isobel, I've got to clear this line. I'm sending Harold for you. He'll be there in an hour."

"Send Fred. Victor, send Fred. At least send Fred."

"Isobel, Fred's at the office. This is a business day. Fred is not a chauffeur. Businesses don't run by themselves."

"Well, will you at least call George? For me? Just call him."

"Speaking of calls, Isobel, I thought I told you in Paris to tell your friends to keep their mouths shut. Hazel called Barney and Barney got right on the phone—" He glanced at Lieutenant Schamper. "Isobel, I want to clear the phone."

"Victor, I'm terribly worried about Gary."

"Isobel," he said in a soft voice, heavy with control, "I'll see you here. It's imperative we keep the phone clear. Please try to understand."

"Victor?"

"Isobel, please. Try to understand." Feldman hung up the phone and exchanged glances with Schamper and Peseta.

17

"Put that goddamn beer away!"

"What the hell're you talking about?"

"You gotta go call Feldman. You won't be able to think straight."

"How about letting me worry about that?"

Roy twisted the cap off the bottle he had just taken from the refrigerator.

Harry walked over to him and, catching him by surprise, snatched the bottle out of his hand. "You've had two or three already. It's about time to go call Feldman. You need everything you've got going for you."

Roy's face went into its characteristic half-smile, a look that revealed his not-too-subtle computer at work. Satisfaction now, or wait. Swing now, or let it ride. Get him now, or get him later. His eye took on its metallic glint. He didn't make a habit of letting people snatch beers out of his hand. He wanted to strike back, to make swift retaliation and recovery, to give full leash to his sense of animal reaction.

But he didn't. His lumbering computer sorted the data and advised against action. He tightened both hands on the edge of the kitchen counter he was leaning against and broadened his smile. "Harry, as long as you been working for me, don't you know by now beer don't affect me? Christ, don't you remember two weeks ago I put those two universal joints in the Ford station wagon? Remember? I was working while you were studying your maps. I musta had twelve beers that afternoon it was so hot and I didn't drop one bearing. You call that being affected by beer? Christ, most guys when they're stone cold sober can't get a set of universals on without spilling the bearings all over the lousy floor."

Harry had followed all the machinations of Roy's mind. He had sensed the decision for restraint. He had gambled on it but felt he had long odds in his favor. Harry figured the odds on most things pretty carefully, made studied estimates and usually had a fair idea of level of risk. Having lived with Roy for a year, he had a complete book on him. Things looked pretty safe for taking the beer from Roy. It might have been different had Roy already finished a few more beers.

He also knew Roy could assemble, disassemble or install universal joints in a complete drunken stupor because Roy was a master automobile mechanic who could do familiar procedures, even tedious ones, almost by instinct. But making the all-important phone call to Feldman required an entirely different kind of skill, and ability to remember details and use them while thinking quickly on his feet, an all-out alertness that would unquestionably be dulled by alcohol.

"You can save this baby till you get back," Harry said. He fished the screw cap out of the sink and tightened it onto the bottle. He opened the refrigerator and placed it back inside. "She'll stay nice and cold and fresh and be waiting for you when you get back." Harry smiled. "That is, if I don't drink it myself."

Roy appeared to go along with the air of levity. "It'll pay you not to touch that one," he piped.

"When you call, you gotta sound different from the way you sounded when you pulled that stupid-ass trick this morning. Change your voice. Bring it down low. Don't let 'em connect it with the person who walked up to the door this morning. Cover the mouth with your hand. Don't use any phone more than one minute because they can probably lock in fast. Stick to the phone route in the book. Start with the one on the parkway. And remember, change your voice. Sound like somebody else."

"They ain't gonna connect the two voices."

"If they do, you'd better start being awful nice to that kid in the other room."

"Harry, you go make the calls. I'll stay here."

"We stick to the book."

"Looks to me like it's time we made a change. You said yourself if they recognize my voice, they can zero in. What do you wanna take that kind of chance for? You make the calls."

"All things considered, we stick to the book."

"It don't make no sense, Harry. You afraid I'll

hurt the kid? You got me convinced we gotta put him on the phone one time."

Now Harry's computer was racing, weighing the risks in each of the two alternatives. He studied Roy's expression for a clue, a positive clue. Roy was half smiling. Harry riffled back through the countless times he had seen that expression. He could leave and come back and find a dead child. He tried to get a handle on Roy's expression. A positive handle. The stony look was back in Roy's eye. He thought of the ease with which they could point a finger by connecting his voice to the license plate. Then he thought of Secaucus and the pigs.

Harry dried his face on his shirt shoulder. "When you use the phone, put a rag over the mouth. And, chrissakes, change your voice. Keep it down. Don't sound so much like a goddamn canary."

Roy's face was rock-hard again. "Whatsa matter, Harry? Losing your guts?" he said in his high, piping voice.

"Just wanta stay alive, pal."

"What time do I leave?"

"Half an hour."

"Then I got time for my baby. Right? Scuse me." Roy moved past Harry to the refrigerator and took out his beer. He removed the loose cap and started drinking.

Harry noted Roy's expression, quickly catalogued it and chose not to comment further.

18

"Let me speak to Mr. Feldman."

"This is Victor Feldman."

"We want two hundred grand for your kid."

"Is the child all right?"

"He is now. He stays that way if you cooperate."

"Let me talk to Gary. Let me hear the child's voice."

"This is going to be a short conversation, Feld-man, and it's going to be about money. You better shut up and listen."

"How do I know my child is still alive?"

"Feel like gambling, Feldman?" Roy sensed that his voice was drifting upward toward its normal range, and he abruptly dropped it on "Feldman."

"If you'd just let me hear his voice, I'll cooperate with you. Just let me hear his voice. That's all I ask."

"Later, Feldman, but not now. Now we talk about money. We want two hundred grand, Feldman. And you got it."

Feldman hesitated. "I didn't expect you to want

so much. I have fifty thousand in cash ready to give you. The money is unmarked."

"We want two hundred, Feldman."

"It's past banking hours. My bank is closed. And it's closed until Monday. I couldn't possibly raise that much money before next week. I have this fifty thousand ready to give you. I will cooperate with you. Please don't harm the child."

"You're stalling, Feldman." Roy hung up. He got back into his car, driving ten minutes or so across town to the second of the phone booths he and Harry had selected in preparing the book. Two teen-age boys were jammed into one of the booths, one talking but both listening. The other was dark. Roy sat in his car and watched the booths. A man drove up, parked and went into the other booth. Roy slumped to appear disinterested, to appear to be waiting to meet someone. He wondered who the man might be and what kind of call he was making. Maybe the guy had grabbed a kid and was coming to place a call. Why not? Good clean work and it pays well.

The two teen-age boys left, and Roy decided to take the booth and hold it until the man left. He went in and sat quietly, waiting for the man to finish. The man hadn't grabbed some kid. Hardly. The man was trying to make a story believeable to his wife. Pitiful son of a bitch!

The man left. Roy adjusted the rag over the phone and dialed. Feldman answered again. "Feldman?"

"This is Victor Feldman."

"We'll take the fifty on account."

112

"Will you return the child then?"

"Wait and see."

"The child is not well. He's a very sick child. He is in desperate need of medication, of medical attention."

"Put some medicine in with the money."

"You're kind of difficult to do business with, whoever you are."

"Wanta to business, Feldman? You're our only customer. If we can't sell you, we get rid of the merchandise." He again adjusted his voice downward in the middle of his dialogue.

"If you'll just let me hear the child's voice, I'll do whatever you say."

"Plan to drop the money tomorrow. You'll hear him before then."

"When?"

"Before then!" His voice was high again.

"But when?"

"You're stalling, Feldman," Roy said and hung up. He got back in his car and drove to another extremity of town in another direction. He went to the next preselected phone booth, some six or so miles from the previous one. Feldman answered again. "Feldman?"

"This is Victor Feldman."

"Deliver the money alone, Feldman. Tomorrow. Take Route Two Fifty-two exactly two and a quarter miles past where it crosses One Forty-four at the shopping center. You'll see a place to pull off the road and you'll see two phone booths there. There's picnic tables and trash cans. You go in the right-hand phone at exactly four o'clock. I'll tell you then where to go with the money. Have it ready in a plain grocery bag. A plain grocery bag. Got the details straight?"

"When will I hear from the boy?"

"Before then."

"When?"

"You like the boy?" Roy said in a sudden bogus-bass voice.

Feldman stammered. "What kind of question is that?"

"Then do like I said."

"Will you return the child then?"

"That's our business. Maybe we'll keep him while we spend some of the money. Just to make sure there's nothing wrong with it. Understand what I mean?"

"How do I know you'll return him after I give you the money?"

"Feel like gambling, Feldman? And, Feldman: No cops. No airplanes. No helicopters. Just you and the money. We'll be watching you. Understand what I mean? You'll be watched all the way. We got walkie-talkies, Feldman. And we'll be watching every step you make."

"Then will you return the boy?"

"Don't forget we were asking two hundred. Even if we decide to sell cheap, we still might panic easy, so don't upset us, Feldman." Roy hung up. He got back in his car and started back to the house.

Feldman put down the phone and looked around the room at the several men. The slightest wisp of a smile played across his face as he glanced at Fred. Then turning to Lieutenant Schamper, who had monitored the call, "It appears they will be willing to accept the fifty thousand, Lieutenant. What do you think?"

"I didn't know you were planning to bargain with them. I hope it wasn't a mistake. Since they appear to be settling for so much less than planned, they're either few in number, or inexperienced, or both. As he said himself, they'll probably panic easy."

"What was your overall impression, Lieutenant?"

Schamper hesitated. "He sounded pretty jumpy and not concerned about the child's welfare. But that's, of course, the impression he'd want to give. At any rate, I don't think one should take any kind of chance."

"Were you able to get anything on the call? A location or anything?"

"Not much. He wasn't on long enough. He seems to know what he's doing in this respect. I suspect he's using pay booths all over the area. That's the only sensible way. That's the way I would handle it if I were doing it."

"Why don't you go in the kidnap business, Lieutenant? You obviously would be good at it, and it apparently pays well."

"I'm sure I could use the money," Schamper answered with a bland smile, his smile stating clearly that he was only making the standard predictable response in an effort to be polite. Then

115

he said, "We made a tape of the calls. What we can do is rerun it a time or two and see if we can pick up anything."

"*Let me speak to Mr. Feldman.*"

They sat clustered around the machine, staring at the carpet, focusing their senses on the electronic voices coming from the recorder. Peseta sat back and watched the skittering around in the gerbil tank across the room as he listened.

"*How do I know my child is still alive?*"

"*Feel like gambling, Feldman?*"

Clenching his eyes shut, Schamper concentrated on the way the high-pitched voice dropped on the word "Feldman."

"*It's past banking hours. My bank is closed. . . .*" Schamper glanced up at Feldman as these words played back.

"*You're stalling, Feldman.*"

The lieutenant looked around from Feldman to Peseta, ready to comment on an observation. While he was hesitating, the tape reached the second of the three phone conversations.

"*We'll take the fifty on account.*"

Schampter looked up at Feldman, who wore a distinctly satisfied expression.

"*If we can't sell you, we get rid of the merchandise.*"

That change in inflection again. What was there about the high-pitched voice occasionally dropping into the bass range and then drifting slowly back up?

"*You're stalling, Feldman.*"

Schamper glanced at Feldman who seemed to

116

be enjoying his own elocution more than he was listening analytically. "There's something about that voice—" Schamper said.

"Sounds like that mechanic to me," Peseta said. Schamper looked at him. "What mechanic?"

"The one this morning. The one looking for Fernhill Drive."

"Feel like gambling, Feldman? And, Feldman: No cops. No airplanes. . . ."

Schamper and Feldman locked glances. "Of course. Of course," Schamper said, getting up. "The guy at the door here this morning."

"The one with the stench," Feldman said.

The lieutenant walked over to the phone, eased the receiver off and dialed a number. "If this turns out," he said, waiting for an answer, "wouldn't that be something?" He shook his head slowly from side to side.

"Well, what have we here, a recording session? Where are the musicians?"

Feldman and the two policemen looked up at the man standing in the door. He wore a golf shirt under a blue blazer and held a small leather doctor's bag in his right hand. He had a rich tan and an athlete's presence. He leaned on his left shoulder against the doorframe.

"Oh, hello, George," Feldman said. "What the hell are you doing here?"

19

"Where's Isobel?"

"Have you tried her hotel in Paris?" Feldman answered.

"She called me and asked me to meet her here about now. She called from JFK."

"And you tore yourself away from the club just for that?"

"It wasn't easy. I'm in the quarter finals of the Pro-Am. We're supposed to play it this afternoon. But you know how it is when Isobel calls. If I don't rush right over, Gary's symptoms have often cleared up before I get here."

"Sorry to disappoint you this time, George. I'm afraid you came for nothing. Gary never felt better, and he's away for the day."

"And I take it these gentlemen are from the police. Gentlemen," Berman said, diverting his attention to them and holding out his hand, "my name is George Berman. I'm Gary's pediatrician."

"Bob Peseta, Doctor," said Peseta, walking over to shake with him. "And Lieutenant Ed Schamper," he said, pointing at Schamper, who was on the phone and about to make contact. Schamper waved a greeting and then began talking quietly into the phone, his small pocket notebook open in his hand.

"I take it Isobel told you," Feldman said.

"I'm not sure what she expected me to be able to do, but for her peace of mind I felt I should be here when she asked me to. She's not home yet?"

"No."

"Any word from Gary or whoever's holding him?"

"Just now."

"Did they put Gary on?"

"No."

"Did they say anything about his condition?"

"No."

"There's no question that this kind of incident could certainly cause his thing to flare up. In fact, it could reach extremely serious porportions. I brought a refill for his nebulizer. I don't know quite how to propose getting it to him, but should the opportunity arise. . . ." Berman wore loafers with wood-hard leather heels. As he stood, he tended to shift his stance, making dull thumps on the carpeted floor with his heels. It was a part of his casual, this-is-the-new-look-for-doctors image. His business car was a convertible. "What did they say about Gary? Did they say anything at all?"

"They said that if I wanted him to remain healthy, I should give them a great deal of money."

Berman grinned. "Well, you've heard that before. I say that to you all the time."

This line touched Feldman in a favorable way. He nodded, smiled a genuinely friendly smile and said, "Yes, you do."

Schamper hung up the phone and jotted a few words into his small notebook. "Our man at the door this morning apparently *was* a mechanic, Mr. Feldman. We ran a check on the tags on the car he was driving. The car belongs to a Roy Walls, who owns a Westside Garage in town. His description, according to his driver's license, more or less fits the man at the door. Our friends at the bureau are following up on this. There are a couple of details about him, though—"

"For instance," Feldman snapped, like a commissioner.

"To begin with," Schamper said, ignoring Feldman's tone, "in our first follow-up on him, we find that he closed his shop and checked out of his apartment a few days ago to go on an extended vacation. I suppose there could be a perfectly good reason why he's still around town and still fixing automobiles. If we could catch up with him to ask him. And the other detail—he has a mechanic workng for him who has a rather lengthy criminal record. Done time twice. Armed robbery, breaking and entering, that sort of thing. A man named Harry Banner."

But Feldman did not hear the name. The front door had opened, and there had been a burst of confusion, the scurrying tat-tat-tat of a woman's heels in the entry foyer. "Victor? Victor? Where is

120

everybody?" Before anyone could respond, she appeared in the door of the room. "Oh, Victor." She ran to him and embraced him briefly. She turned and embraced Berman. "George, thank you for coming." She looked at the other two men. "You must be the police." She paused and looked around at all of them. "My poor baby! . . . Victor, have you heard anything yet? From Gary? From the kidnappers?"

"They just made contact, Mrs. Feldman," Schamper said.

"What about Gary? Is he all right?"

"They asked for money," Feldman said. "Judging from the conversation we just had with them, I would have to guess that Gary is all right. I really feel he's safe and that they'll return him."

She turned back to Feldman to embrace him again. "Oh, Victor, I'm so terribly frightened. This is so inhuman of them to do this to that poor baby."

Feldman said, "I think he's all right. I really do." He returned her embrace. "The conversation is all on tape. Would you like to hear it?" He looked at Peseta to ask him to play the tape and, being unable to think of a name by which to address him, turned to Schamper. "Lieutenant, do you think we might be able to run the tape again?"

20

. . . it's beginning to take shape. Hell, yes. Look at those little pointed ears. Christ, yes, you can really make 'em out. In fact, they're pretty good. And the eyes. Not bad. Big and round. Not bad at all. And right in the right place. Hell, yes. It's taking shape. Really beginning to look like something. Got to narrow it in down here around the feet. Jesus, that'll take some cutting. . . .

. . . so oak's hard. Who's in a hurry? What we got is time. What better time to start a whittling career than when you're waiting? Waiting. Waiting the son of a bitch out. Good hobby when you need a hobby. Takes your mind off of what's on your mind. Keeps your head cool while you think about it. Lets you think about something without thinking about it. Yeah. Funny. Almost as funny as that stupid moron I picked for a partner. Christ, I shoulda took my time. Found somebody else. How many times did I go over it with him? Every detail but one. Who woulda thought you'd have to lecture him on that? . . .

. . . and he had to swallow it. Gobble like a goddamn turkey. All I have is fifty, the man says. And my bank is closed. Christ, banks open for this man. He probably owns the bank. All I have is fifty. Jesus, what a laugh. So what does my partner say? Okay, we'll take fifty now. What does he think we're going to do? Go on playing house here until we get the payoff in installments? Installment buying? Use our easy layaway plan? "Ouch!" Son of a bitch! I gotta be careful not to cut so deep. This knife's too little. Almost cut my goddamn finger off. Bleed, you bastard! Go ahead. . . .

. . . this was gonna be it. My life's work. Planning. Planning. A few days' good, clean, harmless work and take my hands outa gasoline forever. But split fifty and whadda ya got? Twenty-five? How long's that gonna last? Split two hundred and it'll last ya awhile. Shoulda asked three. The man's got it. Christ, he coulda managed five with no trouble. . . .

. . . so what does the moron do? First he drops in for a little visit so they know who he is. Then, when the man says fifty, he says, swell, give us the fifty, and we'll think it over. He says they'll never recognize his voice over the phone. It stands to reason they traced him after he went driving up there this morning with his own plates. They'd be crazy not to. They got nothing else. And that takes 'em right to his landlady. And she says he left town to go on a huntin' vacation. Huntin'. Yeah, huntin'. Huntin' what? Question now is, how long is it gonna take 'em before they point a finger at me? Not long. Cops are only cops, but they can ask questions. It don't take much to put that much together. Next question. How long is it gonna take 'em to run *this* place down? That's a good question. . . .

. . . so with a screwed-up mess like he made out of it, how do you play it? Take the fifty and run like hell? Not much time. We gotta get the kid back and get things the hell outa here. And be on the books with a federal rap. For what? For a lousy twenty-five. I was never gonna work again. This was the big one. My life's work. My career. My masterpiece. That son of a bitch in the living room. My partner. He blows the whole thing all to hell. Drives right up to the door. His own plates. I shoulda made the calls. Taken the kid with me to the phone. Anything but let that brain trust in there handle it. Disguise his voice? Christ, he can't even talk regular. Sounds like some kind of a goddamn bird. Then goes driving up to the door. Chirping like a bird. Right up to the door. His own plates. . . .

. . . got to be some way to save this whole thing. Take the twenty-five and run and we'll still have to start all over before long. Can't ever come back here. Have to change everything. Harry Banner is a dead man. A dead man. Twenty-five ain't enough for that. Got to get more some way. Got to make this job pay. Big payoff once and for all. Got to make it worth having to change everything. Jesus, my finger hurts. Softer wood next time. That much he's right about. . . .

. . . there's got to be a way. Maybe use the kid

some way. Get him to help me. Christ, he's smarter than bird-brain in there. Poor, sick little son of a bitch. Shoulda put *him* on the phone. He probably wouldn'ta blew it so bad. Good little kid. Gotta figure out some way to use him. But it's gotta shape up fast. Cops are bad, but not stupid. The kid'll work with me. Christ, he loves me. I got him in my pocket. I start talking about taking him to California and I thought he was gonna blow up. Nice little kid. First-class. I just gotta figure out how to do something with him. . . .

. . . tomorrow's everything. Tonight we put the kid on the phone. Birdbrain won't give me no trouble till after that. Even he sees that much. But tomorrow. Things are gonna happen fast. Gotta get out of this place. The cops got the bureau helping 'em. They got to find it before long. Gotta get outa here. Gotta keep the kid on my side. Gotta keep Roy away from the kid. Gotta think of something. Some way to get some more out of this. Awful small payday for what we bought ourselves. Send him back to the phone? Tell Feldman we want more money by the payoff? It's no use. Too late. He might screw things up worse. It's gonna be busy tomorrow. We're gonna sweat it as it is. There's gotta be some way, though. Wonder what time it is? . . .

. . . look at them shavings. Not bad. That's a lot of shavings for this knife. And oak. Must be time to eat. He'll be coming in here in a minute looking for his meal. . . .

21

"Looks like you got what was coming to you try-ing to cut oak with that little toothpick there, pal."

Harry didn't answer.

"Hope you didn't lose too much blood."

Harry continued to whittle in silence, trying to round off a sharp corner with small, helpless, scraping motions. He turned the blade almost flat against the wood to take a cut. The blade headed in too deeply, balked and almost nicked him again.

Roy snickered. "Why don't you rest up from that for a while and do something you do a little better, like fix us something to eat?"

"Anything on the TV? Any kinda mention of anything?"

"Nothing. How about fixing something to eat? I'm hungry." Roy opened the refrigerator and took out another bottle of beer.

"Get three of those dinners out of there and we'll start heating 'em up."

Roy opened the freezer compartment and took out three TV dinners. He dropped them on the table in front of Harry and closed the refrigerator. He opened the beer and took a double gulp.

Harry put the knife and wood in his pocket and got up. He slipped the aluminum trays out of the boxes and put them in the oven. He gave the temperature knob a twist, paying little attention to the setting.

Roy slid onto a chair and set his bottle and elbows on the table. "Harry?"

The tone of Roy's "Harry" said that Roy wanted to have a little quiet, serious, reasoning, earnest discussion. Harry sat back down. It was time to try setting something up.

"Harry, you gotta listen the way I been thinking this thing out. I been sitting there all day, thinking this thing out, and it's clear. There's a way to come out and a way to go under, and I figure out what gives the best percentage on each. And now you gotta listen."

"Why don't you get me a beer?"

Roy took this as a move on Harry's part to get something out of him, to win a hand, to make room to give a little without looking like an all-out loser. He got up and got a beer out of the refrigerator. He twisted the bottle top off and set the beer in front of Harry. Then he sat back down, took an oversize swallow of his own beer and studied Harry as he got the swallow under control. "Harry, the way I see it, you're planning to get caught. You're a two-timer already and you got a losin' attitude. You're looking out now to make things as easy for yourself as you can after they pick you up. The way I see it, if you think this way, the odds are all in favor of your going under. Getting picked up."

Harry was fascinated. He was seeing a Roy Walls he had never seen before. But it was a Roy he had sensed was going to emerge the moment Roy had indicated that he wanted to talk. It was a calm, thoughtful, analytical, almost scholarly Roy. But it was also a predictable Roy. He was going to hear the same arguments, the same point of view Roy had taken since they picked up the kid. This time, however, it was all going to be presented, not in his usual, like-I-say-or-screw-you style, but in a restrained, organized way, the only way Roy could figure he had a chance of being persuasive. It was an opening, a setup, a chance to let Roy convince him. It was a way to lull Roy to sleep for a while till he could think of something. But he had to be careful not to be too easy. He had to put up enough resistance to keep Roy from smelling that bait was bait. He had to play him like a big fish.

"You see, Harry, you're thinking too much about protecting yourself in case you lose. When you think about losing, you lose. I play to win. I been thinking all afternoon about how we play it to win. There's no second place, pal. It's win it all or lose it all.

"Now let's talk about winning," Roy continued. "There's only one link between us and grabbing the kid, and that's the kid himself. Now I don't care what you say, pal. But you know it and I know it. The only thing connecting us to that kid is the kid himself. Say what you want. Get rid of the connecting link and we're clean. Take our money and go away for a while. Everybody that knows us knows we're going away. We go away for a while, and we can even come back. But if we leave that kid around, we got to spend the rest of our life waiting for him to point 'em at us. It's simple, pal. Night and day. He's the one link."

"Roy. How stupid do you think the cops are?"

"It don't make no difference, pal. They got nothing."

"What about the fact that you walked up to the man's door and presented yourself and your own plates?"

"I told 'em I was a mechanic. Everything'll check. The last person in the world they're going to point the finger at is somebody who comes walking up to the door."

"What about the fact that you were supposed to have left town a couple days before?"

"That ain't against the law. Besides, by the time they get around to talking to my landlady, she's too stupid to remember when I left."

"What about the fact that you got a two-timer working for you? And who's got a sister working for the man?"

"You did your time."

"What about the fact—I don't know, Roy."

"It keeps coming up the same way, pal. He's the only link."

"I don't know, Roy. I gotta think it through. You may be right. It may be our only chance of getting out with our necks, but I gotta think it through."

"You do it, pal, and you'll come up with the same answer."

"Maybe. One thing I know. We need the kid on the phone tonight."

Roy took a swallow of his beer. "I go along with that." He said it in the tone of an arbitrator conceding something in return for something gained.

"If we do it, we do it after the pickup."

Roy's expression changed. "Why after the pickup? We're gonna wanta run like hell after the pickup."

Harry suddenly had the sinking feeling that he had blown the whole thing. "Because I got to think about it some more, Roy, and so far, that's the way it looks to me. It ain't gonna be easy for me to do. Maybe after we got the money in our hands and he's between us and getting the hell out clean, maybe I'll feel different. It just won't be easy for me. That's all."

"Don't worry about that part, pal."

"You're doing it is the same as me doing it, and it won't be easy. Lemme think it through. If we do it, we do it after."

Roy took his beer and sat back in his chair. He took another gulp that drained the bottle. "You think it through, pal."

Harry studied Roy's face and tried to get a handle on the expression. That sincere look was gone. The face of the old Roy, the screw-you Roy was back. He felt a little sickened. He felt as if maybe he'd let the big one off the hook. That could just make things even cozier for the next twenty-four hours. Yessir.

22

Harry sat up in bed and looked around. He looked at the clock on the face of the radio but couldn't quite make it out. Leaning closer and squinting, he saw it was a little before four. A good time to go. He wanted very badly to drop back down and continue sleeping, but it was a good time to go. He looked down at the child in the narrow bed with him. The child was sleeping on his side, his feet stuck through the posts of the bed to make the pressure from the handcuffs off his ankles, his breathing quiet and regular.

Harry rubbed his face a couple of times and sat on the side of the bed without moving. He stroked the back of his neck a time or two and then rubbed his face again. After several minutes, he slipped his feet into his shoes, tied them, got up and walked to the door of the room. Tiptoeing as soundlessly as possible, he quietly lifted the chair he had left in front of the bedroom door. He had placed it there and closed the door, assuming he would be warned if Roy came in during the night. He eased the bedroom door open and jumped back, startled, his blood hammering. He had come face-to-face, almost nose-to-nose, with Roy, who stood in a semicrouch, as if ready to spring, an open-eyed, hard-set expression on his face.

"What are you up to?" Harry asked, still trying to catch his breath.

"I was coming to call you. It's getting time to take the kid to the phone. Right?" Roy half smiled.

"I was coming to call you for that," Harry said, his pulse still fast. "But I don't get the feeling that's what you had in mind."

"What else?" Roy said through his sickish grin. "You got the kid tied up and ready to go?"

"Not yet, but it just takes a minute."

They walked into the bedroom, making no effort to be quiet, and turned on the overhead light. The child, seemingly unaware of their entrance, tried to turn over but was restrained by his tiny manacled ankles. He took a deep breath, in and out, the way a child does, the way no adult can do.

Harry sat down on the side of the bed and touched the child on the shoulder. "Wake up, Redhead," he said in a loud whisper. The child took another deep breath and rolled back over onto his side. He smacked his lips a couple of times and mumbled something. Harry gave his little shoulder another firm shake. "Wake up, Redhead." The child was having difficulty waking up into the darkness of the bandage which covered his eyes. "Let's go, Redhead," Harry said. "We're going out and get a little air." He unlocked one side of the handcuffs.

"Where are we going?" The child was still sleepy, still trying to accustom his eyes to being open but seeing nothing.

"We're going out for a ride to use the telephone," Harry said. "Let you talk to your folks."

"Isn't there a phone here?" the child asked.

"It don't work," Roy said quickly.

"We're gonna go use a different phone, Redhead. Take a nice ride. This is the nicest time o' day. Bet you were never out this time o' day." Harry had brought the cuff from around the metal rod in the bed and resnapped it onto the other tiny foot. He picked up the two small shoes and began putting them on. "Wouldn't you like to go out and take a little drive?"

The cross-bandaged face seemed to brighten. "I'd like to get off this bed for a while. I'm sure of that."

"Wouldn't you like to talk to your folks?" Harry asked.

"Sure." The boy shrugged almost indifferently.

"C'mon. I'll carry you." Harry started to pick him up.

"Wait a minute," Roy said, grabbing Harry's arm. "What about his hands and the gag?"

"It's not necessary. Where's he going to go with these cuffs on his legs?"

"Have you lost your mind? Where's he going to ride? Up front, like one of the family?"

"I'm telling you he'll be OK."

"And I'm telling you, he goes in the trunk. We don't know who we'll run into. I don't care if it is the middle of the night."

"I'm telling you we don't have to."

Roy's face was taking on its hard set. "And I'm telling you we're not taking any chances with my neck. You were the one told me how to do things, and we're doing 'em that way."

Harry looked down at the child's taped-up face. "Just take it easy, Redhead. It won't be for but a few minutes." He looked across the room at the desk. "Hand me the rope for his hands," Harry said in a restrained voice.

The child choked up. "Please, don't tape my mouth up the way you did before. I couldn't breath before."

"Put the gag on." There was a brutal chill in Roy's tooting voice.

"There's no need for it," Harry said. "You can drive and I'll sit in back with the kid. I'm telling ya, he won't cause no trouble."

"He goes in the trunk. Suppose a cop stops us for something. You'd look damn silly in back with him and me in front."

"What's he gonna stop us for?"

"I don't know. Any damn thing. This hour of the morning?"

"Well, we'll look damn silly if we start unloading this kid out of the trunk at a phone booth if someone sees us."

Roy hesitated. "Why'd you plan it that way? . . . How're we gonna handle it then?"

Harry indulged himself a brief neck massage.

"We both gotta ride in front. . . . But we can't pull the kid outa the trunk. . . . Someone sees that — We put him on the back-seat. . . . Someone sees that— We put him on the back-seat floor under a blanket."

"Suppose we get stopped. The kid sounds off and we're dead."

"Number one, we're dead anyway if we get stopped, gag or no gag. They'll still hear him if he wants to make a racket. Number two, he won't make a racket. Number three, we won't get stopped. No reason why we should."

"Why don't we just call from here?"

"Some things I don't know about and one of them is how fast they can nail down a telephone. We better use one of our booths we got picked out. Let's use the one out on Eighty."

"Then let's get moving." Roy took the rope and lashed the two small wrists. Then he slipped the end of the rope around the short chain on the handcuffs and drew up, pulling hands and feet together.

"No use twisting him up that way," Harry said.

"I don't want him trying to open the door and jump out."

"Well, don't tie his hands and feet together. If they're both tied, he won't be going anywhere. He'll be harder to handle when we get to the phone booth."

Roy hesitated and then released the strand of rope connecting hands and feet. A trace of smile brightened the boy's face. Roy glanced at his smile and scowled. He reached over to the desk and picked up the adhesive tape. He looked at the helpless child, grabbed the child's hand and touched it to the roll of tape. "Listen, kid, you make a sound when we don't tell you to and I'll tape up the rest of your face for you. That clear?"

"I won't say a word," the boy answered, still smiling.

23

They drove in silence. Harry had laid the child carefully on the floor in the back of the car and covered him with a blanket. The blanket was good. It was cool at that hour for nothing but a polo shirt and play slacks. Harry almost tucked him in when he arranged him and the blanket on the floor. He wadded an end of the blanket as a pillow under the child's head.

The roads were deserted. They met no traffic. They saw perhaps one or two cars. When they arrived at the phone booth on Route 80, it was deserted as expected. Roy pulled up so that the car doors opened directly into the booth. Then he climbed out, stepped into the booth, and without closing the door to avoid turning on the light, dialed the Feldman number. Afer one and a half rings, Feldman answered in an alert voice. "Yes?"

"Feldman?"

"This is Victor Feldman."

"I'm gonna put your kid on."

"Hello! Hello! Gary? Hello!" Another phone

lifted somewhere in the house, and Mrs. Feldman said, "Gary? Are you there? Gary? Gary, my baby!"

Harry had carried the child over to the booth. Roy grabbed the small, tied hands and stuffed the phone into them, lifting it up to the child's ear. "Hello," the child said.

"Gary? Is that you?" said Victor Feldman.

"Gary, are you all right?" said Isobel Feldman.

"My hands are tied and my feet are in real handcuffs, but they didn't put the tape back over my mouth because Banner——" Roy wrenched the phone out of his hand.

"Gary? Gary, where did you go?" said Victor Feldman.

"Gary, do you need medication?" said Isobel Feldman.

"If you ever want to hear his voice again, Feldman, you'll be by that phone this afternoon at four. And ready with the money."

"Don't harm the child and I'll be there," said Victor Feldman.

"We'll put some medication in with the money," said Isobel Feldman. "He can't be without his medication. It's very important."

"Just do as you're told or he won't need any medicine."

"Wait, wait," said Victor Feldman. "Can't you let the child talk to his mother a little? Be a reasonable man."

"Please," said Isobel Feldman.

"Four o'clock." Roy hung up. Then he looked at Harry with icy contempt. "You hear what the kid said! He told 'em your name! I warned you, goddammit! He told 'em your name! That's what you get for getting so friendly with the kid."

Harry's face took its characteristic resigned set. "I think you grabbed the phone in time. I don't think they picked it up."

"There were cops listening in, too. I think we just screwed the whole job."

"We've got Feldman in our pocket. He's not going to let the cops do much of anything till he pays the money and gets the kid. Our best bet is to stay cool and hold onto our aces. The kid is our ace. Besides, I don't think they picked it up." Harry was holding the child in front of him, gripping one of the tiny shoulders in each hand. He picked him up and placed him back on the floor of the car, covering him with the blanket.

They got back into the car and drove off, driving in silence. When they had driven for about fifteen minutes, Harry said, "Look out for that one."

The child wondered if they had seen a police car. He suddenly felt very frightened by what the effects of his mistake might prove to be. He wondered if all the plans would be changed. He wondered if he was still safe with Banner. How far were they from the police car, if that was what it was? Maybe he should jump up and scream for help. No. It was probably too far away. No. Stick with Banner. Banner would handle everything.

24

"I trust you slept well."

"Seconal," she answered, without looking at him. She was wearing a tailored short-sleeved dressing gown over something knee-length, of very sheer nylon.

Victor Feldman cut a trim square of his thick ham steak and, using his knife, piled some scrambled egg on top of it. "It's nice having you back home." A bad line. He regretted having said it. "I wish something more"—he shrugged—"something more pleasant had brought you home early." Another regrettable line. Who was he trying to kid? He put the carefully constructed bite of ham and egg into his mouth as he studied her quiet expression and downward glance. She really wasn't an unattractive woman. Even in the morning. Even after last night. Hardly a night of beautifying rest.

Her orange juice had settled slightly. She took a teaspoon and stirred it. "Oh, good morning,

Sara," she said when the cook appeared, having come in to freshen Feldman's coffee.

"You all right?"

"Oh, sure." She managed a warm smile for her friend, her dedicated friend for a good number of years.

"Fix you some breakfast? You like some coffee now?"

"I think I'd just like tea and toast."

"You sure you all right?"

"That really is what I would like to have." She smiled again. "And I feel fine. I promise."

"All right, then." Sara went toward the kitchen.

She looked at her husband, who was smearing butter on a small chunk of danish. "I really feel rotten," she said. "Having taken the sleeping pill and then having gotten up for their phone call. But at least I thought Gary sounded okay. Didn't you think he sounded all right? I was terribly drugged. But I'm sure it was him. Don't you agree it was Gary?"

"No doubt about that." He was grateful for her question. It gave him something easy to say.

"I wish they would have let me talk with him longer. There was so much I wanted to find out from that poor child. So much I wanted to tell him."

"They only want you to know he's alive."

"But I'm his mother."

Feldman nodded.

"But he did sound as if they were not hurting him or anything like that. And he sounded well. I mean, I would have expected him to be in terrible need of George. But somehow he didn't sound that way at all."

"No, thank God, he sounded very well." Listen to *me*.

"I'll feel so much better when we have him back home. I don't dare even consider the possibility that they won't return him and without harm as soon as you take them the money this afternoon."

"He should be back home tonight." He tried to say it with comforting assurance.

"Oh, Victor, perhaps—" She paused.

He didn't dare look up from his plate, where he was constructing another bite-sized edifice of egg on ham.

"Sometimes things can, well"—she hated to use a cliché, but she couldn't think of a good substitution that said the same thing—"happen for the best."

He took the bite and chewed silently, still avoiding her eyes.

"Sometimes it takes a crisis to make people stop and think, to make people realize things they know but won't let themselves think about."

He wished she were still in bed.

"Don't you agree, Victor, that some good could come from this? Don't you agree that sometimes people grow a little when faced with mutual adversity, when they have to face something . . . together? Sometimes a crisis can—"

Sara came in with a pot of tea and a dish of toast. "More coffee, please, Sara," Feldman said. He glanced at Isobel and then dropped his eyes back to his plate. Here we go again. She never gives up, this girl. So very delicately she reaches out. So refined, so restrained, so controlled. . . . It was sobering—wasn't it, my dear?—to have someone walk into your house and walk away with your child, your only child, your precious *redheaded* child that you love and protect so endearingly from thousands of miles away. But somehow, my handsome woman, although I would like to oblige, although I would like to respond, I just don't seem to want to. "This is very good coffee. Excellent coffee."

"Victor, don't you think that sometimes a crisis can help make people see things more clearly?"

"Your toast is getting cold. Would you like some danish? This is delicious danish." Last night and again this morning. She really, honestly wants. . . . Why, it was the first time she'd undressed in my presence in months. . . . Not undress, though —with her it's more disrobe. . . . I really should have responded to your overture, my sweet. Who am I to pass up so appealing an opportunity? You're still quite lovely. And I must admit you've got class. Real class. No mention of *her*. And so tasteful in your approach, your manner, your breeding. Nothing overt. As if it was just as it has always been. But I'm afraid nothing happened. Not a tremor. I'm sorry, but that was the way it was. I'm sorry that I sent you to the medicine chest for one of your little pink capsules. Would you want me to be insincere? Would you want me to live a lie?

"No, Victor, I don't want any danish. Victor . . . don't you think that sometimes a crisis can . . . bring people back together?"

There. She said it. She finally got it out. He forced himself to look up. "I certainly do. Our mutual crisis brought you quickly home so that we could face this thing together. I must say, I marvel at the quickness with which you got back from so far away."

"Oh, Victor." This time *she* looked down. She filled her cup, added a pinch of sugar, a splash of cream, and stirred. She began buttering a triangle of toast.

He took another swallow of coffee and then brought his napkin to his lips. Surely there had been many moments of crisis throughout history that did not lead to scenes of dramatic reconciliation. Surely there must have been cases of poor communication even in covered wagons. Another overture ignored. Another option passed up. Why does it hurt more each time instead of less? At any rate there's no point in lingering in a painful situation. "I'll be in the library. I've some . . . things to work on."

She didn't even look up as he left the table.

25

Victor Feldman left before three. The money was in tight bundles, taped and neatly stacked in a large fresh kraft-paper bag with chain-super-market advertising imprinted on it. The bag was at his side on the car seat, the top of the bag folded down three or four times and taped. He had allowed plenty of time, perhaps a half hour more than needed, based on the police estimate of the driving time to the parking area on Route 252, two or so miles past the shopping center. Schamper had suggested police surveillance of his car as far as the shopping center, but he had insistently forbidden it, choosing to stick strictly to the instructions laid out by the kidnappers, his instinct telling him that things were going pretty much his way. Let the police and their friends from the FBI work below the surface. Fine. But not out in the open.

As he drove, he began playing back his experiences over the last forty-eight hours, rehashing, rearranging, planning how he would execute a perfect kidnapping. He thought of his often stated business philosophy: "Show me what you do, and if I like it, I'll take your business away from you." He had gotten into the importing business this way and had expanded his empire along all sorts of tangents by practicing this business philosophy, meeting others in lines not too unlike his, discussing the subtleties of their specific lines and then making a carefully calculated move into their sphere.

Kidnapping was a game that was certainly subject to sound business strategy. He amused himself as he drove, considering the pros and cons of various tactical maneuvers, examining countless variations on the plan the kidnappers had used, weighing the risks in each. But as he played this little thought game, he kept coming back to the smirking conclusion that only submoron types would resort to anything so stupid as overt crime to make money when money was so easy to make.

Submorons. A sobering thought. They probably were, in fact, submorons. When one deals with submorons, it is important not to startle or provoke them since they might react like animals. So far they were behaving, following along acceptable lines. Good. But careful! Nothing sudden or unexpected. Quiet, sure manipulation. Fifty was certainly an improvement over two hundred. It appeared the kidnappers were disposed to settling early. By quiet, sure manipulation he had induced them to accept quite a reduction in committed funds.

The next step was another judicious compromise. An attractive consideration to both parties to the negotiation. He would trade removal of the heat on them, the vicious snapping of police dogs at their rumps, for safe return of the child, no questions asked. The note was in with the money. It was certainly a bargain. Then he would capitulate to the demands of the law and allow the police to recover what they could of the moneys still outstanding. He made a mental note to check with his accountants on how losses in ransom money are handled, tax-wise.

"It's time," Harry said.

"Why don't we call from here?"

"Don't start."

"Why not? That phone booth on the side of the highway is not like Feldman's house. Christ, they can't do anything with it."

"You lost your mind, Roy? They've known what phone booth we're gonna call into for twenty-four hours now. God knows what they can do with that. Stick to the book. Place your call and get the hell away from the phone you're using. Keep it short and keep your voice down."

Roy reached in his pocket and pulled out a scrap of paper with two phone numbers on it. He refolded it and slipped it back into his pocket. Then he glanced at his watch. "Hell, I've got plenty of time."

"You ain't got plenty of time. It's past three, nearly a quarter after. Driving time to the place you leave the car is nearly twenty minutes. Then it's fifteen minutes' walking to the phone booth. You gotta allow spare time. You're cutting it close already."

Roy hesitated. "Why don't you go this time? I'll stay here and take care of the kid."

"*Jesus, Roy! This is it! The Payoff! Now will you please go?*"

Roy made a half snort, a noisy gesticulation that expressed his distaste for repeatedly taking instructions from Harry. Then he started across the kitchen for the basement door.

"Remember," Harry said. "After you talk at four, it'll take him about twenty minutes' driving to get to the car. Then wait twenty more minutes after he leaves before you go to the car, just in case. And stay outa sight." Harry followed Roy into the hall.

Roy opened the basement door.

"Got plenty of change?" Harry asked.

Roy paused, put his right hand in his pocket, pulled out a fat handful of nickels, dimes and quarters. For a moment he considered throwing the money at Harry's face. Then he eased it back into his pocket and started down the steps.

"Take it easy," Harry said.

Roy hesitated on the second step and then went on.

Feldman arrived at the phone booths at twenty to four. He parked facing the booths, which were empty. He glanced at his watch and then at the clock on the dash. They checked to less than two minutes. He snapped on the radio to a local station to wait for another time check.

He glanced around at the terrain and then began nodding his head in approval. It was a good spot for the call. Two phones and an almost negligible likelihood that both would be busy at a given time. A desolate spot, yet in a nice little valley. Good elevated points for observation all around. Quite good. Nice cover. Good vegetation. The kidnappers had done some careful planning. Too bad he didn't want to try kidnapping. Perhaps he might have hired them to do some of the detail work. One of the prerequisites for efficient pursuit of the dollar is hiring the right man for the right job. He could have Fred put these men, whoever they were, through the personnel bit: "Fred, would you call our psychological consultants and have them test these gentlemen for skills pertinent to kidnapping?"

Roy pulled the Chevy to a stop and hopped out. He locked the door and glanced at the buttons on the other doors to be sure they were locked. He ran his finger along the top edge of the window, driver's side. Open just a crack. Then he glanced at his Timex. Jesus! It was cutting it close. Maybe the son of a bitch was fast. Hell, it was right. He'd have to move. Quicker'n hell.

He went to the front of the car and pulled out the snap fasteners holding the license plate.

Carrying the plate, he went to the rear of the car and took off the other one. The fasteners in his left hand and the plates under his left arm, he rummaged in his right-hand pocket to get the car keys back out. His fingers touched the change, plenty of change, and then the string with the key to the cuffs. He smiled. Harry never knew when he copped it. He saw the chance and grabbed it. Harry wouldn't need it before he got back. Course not. What possibly for? If the kid had to piss, he'd just have to hold it a little while, that's all. How long would he be gone? Two hours altogether? The kid could wait.

He finally fished out the key chain with the car keys. Unlocking the trunk, he lifted the mat, grabbed another pair of license plates, dropped them on the ground and then placed the plates from the car under the mat. He brought the trunk door down with a harsh slam and checked it. Locked. Picking the plates up off the ground, he installed them, looked around in all directions, glanced at his Timex again and then started off down the road on foot. He walked a few paces and stopped. The trunk key! He ran back, opened the hood, took a key off the chain and laid it on the air cleaner. Closing the hood, he glanced at his watch and then broke into a trot.

He suddenly felt very hot. He checked his Timex again and then sped up, almost to a dead run, wiping his face on his shoulder and mumbling a chain of high-pitched, barely audible profanities as he ran.

"Whadda ya say, Redhead?"

The child was lying relaxed, his hands behind his head, staring into the nothingness of his taped eyes. He turned his head at the sound of Harry entering the room.

"This is it, Redhead. We hit the road."

"No fooling?" The excited child sat himself up and turned his head in Harry's direction.

"Now, would I kid you? What've I been telling you all along? Yes, sir, you do everything just like I tell you and, Jesus, there's no limit . . ." Harry sat down on the edge of the bed. "First thing, let's take the tape off the eyes." He began fumbling with the crossed ends extending below the child's ears. "First, I'm going to teach you how to borrow cars. Hey, this tape's not too terribly tight right here."

"What's to learn about borrowing cars? You just ask if you can borrow it and then they lend it to you." The child shrugged his fragile shoulders.

"Not my way. My way, you don't ask, you just borrow."

"Oh?" The child sensed the light tone of Harry's voice. "OK, how do you do it?"

"You gotta be able to smell from a pretty good distance away if the key's been left in a car."

"Yeah? How do you do that?"

"It takes experience, Redhead, lots of experience." Harry had the two crosspieces of tape loose to where they cross the strip going over the eyes and around the head. "Then I'm going to show you how to borrow a little money for airplane tickets so we can fly to California."

"Do you borrow that without asking for it, too?"

"Sometimes, if no one's around to ask. And sometimes you ask for it, but you use an agent to help you present your case, you know what I mean? An agent to argue for you."

"What kind of an agent?"

"You hold it in your hand and you aim it at the guy's head that has the money. You know what I mean?"

"I think I understand." The child smiled.

"And you gotta be able to smell when a business establishment is ripe for a little discussion on letting you borrow all their money."

"And that takes experience," the child said.

"You're learning."

"I'll sure be glad when we take the tape off so I can look at your nose that can smell all these things."

"That's the way we'll be working, Redhead. You'll see. We'll fly to California and borrow a little money along the way as we need it."

"Are you going to let me watch you borrow?"

"Remember what I told ya, Redhead. For this whole trip to work out, you gotta do everything I tell you. Understand." Harry pulled the bandage away from the child's eyes, almost with a flourish, as though he were surgeon and the child were patient and it was that moment when they would know if the operation had been a success.

Their eyes met, a prolonged meeting. The child ventured a small smile, like taking a single step into a dark room. Harry smiled. Then the child expanded his smile. Harry grinned broadly. The child grinned, studying Harry's face. "Ol' Banner. Ol' Banner."

"Let's get the cuffs off and get the hell outa here before we run out of time." Harry began exploring his pocket for the string with the key on it. His face clouded. He stood up and concentrated on the search. Emptying the pocket into his hand, he then pulled it inside out, studied the contents of his hand, stuffed it back into his pants and went into the other pocket. "Oh, Jesus! *No!*" He rammed both hands into his back pockets and looked upward, his face tightening into a frown. When? How? How in hell? It didn't fall out. And it didn't walk off. The spilled beer! It had to be the spilled goddamn beer. While the pants were hanging over the kitchen chair and he was walking around in his skivs. Had to be. One minute while he went to take a leak he was not in the room with those pants. And Roy was. One minute. And Roy could know just how much time he had from the noise of the goddamn water.

The child watched Harry's face. "Banner? What's the matter?"

"We just hit a small snag, Redhead. A little matter of the key to the cuffs."

"We don't even need it, Banner." The child, working quickly, untied and removed a shoe, then the sock, and began working his foot out of the cuff. It hurt a little as he rushed, but he got it out and started on the other.

Harry broke into a broad grin and shook his

head from side to side. "Jesus Christ! Jesus H. Christ!" He watched the child snake his other foot out of the locked cuff. "Just leave 'em right there on the bed, boy. Roy'll think we was Houdini. Get your shoes and socks back on and let's haul ass."

Feldman glanced at his watch. Nine minutes, perhaps eight minutes to four. A Saturday afternoon in July. A grocery bag containing fifty thousand dollars. A fee to be paid to some animal so that a man can have his own child continue to live under his own roof. His own redheaded child. His and Isobel's. "Congratulations, Victor." "Thanks, Barney." "I never guessed you'd be the one to get her, somehow, Victor." "She is a lovely woman." "I understand you're going into the business." "I don't think you quite understand, Barney." "What's to understand, Victor? You know I'm not being sarcastic when I say that I have great respect for you. The whole package. Isobel and the family business." "You don't know the facts, Barney." "You're a remarkable man, Victor. You're the only man I know who immigrated in his teens and who has no trace of an accent. No vestige. The king's English, Victor. And now Isobel. And the business." "You don't understand, Barney. *They need me*. We're standing at the threshold of the greatest boom in importing that history has ever seen. And they're about to go under. Can you believe? They're about to go under. They've got everything on paper: established name, pipelines, contacts, everything. And at this moment in history, this moment when the feast is due to begin, they're about to go under. *They need me.*" "And you, Victor?" "Well, certainly I won't deny that in most respects, this is a rare opportunity, a most intriguing opportunity. I can't deny the setup is attractive. But *they need me.*" "And Isobel?" . . .

A car pulled into the parking area. Four teen-age boys. Feldman glanced at his watch. Two minutes to four. Two of the boys, one from the back and one from the front, jumped out of the car and went into the phone booths. They each dropped in money and dialed.

One minute to four. What could this new complication mean? What will the animal do when he dials the phone in the booth and gets a busy signal? He could be shaken. Surely he'll have the good sense to recognize that this could happen. Surely he'll keep trying until the line is clear. Don't be a fool, whoever you are. I have the money here for you. The teen-age boys. Perhaps they're a part of this whole thing. That's a twist. No. Not likely. They haven't even looked over this way. What if they knew that they could walk over here and, on threat of violence, walk away with fifty thousand dollars? I'm glad they don't know.

But they're *watching* me. From some obscure vantage point, they're watching me. They said they would be. Then they will understand about the busy signal. But what if they are watching from such a distance that they don't understand this ordinary car and these four ordinary teen-age boys? From a great distance they see a plain-clothes car and four young plainclothesmen. Hey, animals! Wherever you are, don't do anything rash. The money is here for you. Be patient. The phone can't stay busy forever.

Roy sighted his phone booth and dropped his intermittent trot-run to a walk. His head, in fact, his entire body, throbbed from heat and exhaustion. He had a severe cramp in the calf of his left leg. He was struggling to breathe, his body soaked.

Late. A minute or two. Maybe five. Feldman could wait. He could keep his money a lousy few minutes longer. But he might panic and not follow instructions. Shoulda left earlier. On time. Like Harry wanted him to do. Harry had everything figured. Details all figured. Shoulda stuck to Harry's book and not had to run. . . . What the hell. What's Feldman going to do? What *can* he do? He's got to wait. Let the son of a bitch wait. An hour's one thing. But five minutes? Ten minutes? Let the son of a bitch cry a little, worrying. Harry said impress him by having the phone ring four on the dot. . . . This way's better. Let him sweat it a little, worrying.

He dragged himself into the booth. Collapsing onto the seat, he allowed his body to slump. He closed his eyes and concentrated on breathing. Opening them a moment, he glanced at the service station nearby. Nothing going on. He glanced at his Timex. Seven after. Maybe eight.

He slumped again. Rest. One minute. Two minutes. Gotta rest. Gotta concentrate on what to say. Make it quick. Keep my voice down.

He fought with his damp pocket and damp hand and managed to get some of the change out and drop it on the shelf under the phone. Working his other hand into the other pocket and back out again, he brought out the paper with the numbers. He checked his Timex. Eleven after.

He dropped a dime into the phone and dialed the top number on the paper, the one marked RIGHT. As soon as he heard the busy signal, he brought the receiver down hard on the hook and looked all around him. Dropping in another dime, he studied the scrap of paper. Then he dialed with great concentration. No mistake in dialing this time. He slammed the receiver down again and whimpered. Dropping in still another dime, he dialed the other number, the one marked LEFT, *dialing* with meticulous care. Busy. He slammed the receiver and made a throaty noise, almost a scream, his face contorting. He slammed the base of his fist against one of the wire-reinforced glass panels in the booth, cracking it. Studying the crack pattern a moment, he hit at it again, watching the crack lines lengthen. Then he slumped again and whimpered once more, his face all agony and confusion.

Something had to be wrong. Both lines couldn't be busy. Maybe one, but not both of them. Something was going on. Something stank. Harry! Harry would know what to do. Call Harry. It's Harry's book. Harry thinks of everything.

He dropped another dime in the phone, still ignoring the dimes in the coin return. He started to dial and stopped. What the hell was the number? He read the instructions on the phone and dialed Information.

A feminine voice mumbled something.

"Uh, Esposito on Tarbell Road."

There was a pause. He glanced at his watch. Sixteen after. He felt a sudden flush of heat propagate down through him. The operator gave him the number, and he hung up, put in two nickels and dialed quickly. It was ringing. He took a relaxing breath.

Four rings . . . six, eight, ten. He slumped back with the receiver at his ear. *"Answer it, you son of a bitch!"* he shouted at the top of his voice. He let it ring at great length and then hung up. He slammed his fist again at the cracked glass, this time producing a few splinters. He wiped the base of his fist on his pants leg to remove any glass fragments. Twenty-one after. He wiped his face on his shoulder, put two more nickels in the phone and again dialed the number marked RIGHT. It rang.

"Hello," said a strong voice after one ring.

Roy hesitated and then, like testing bath water with a big toe, tried a small "Feldman?"

"This is Victor Feldman."

Roy wiped his face again and looked all around him. "You alone?"

"Aren't you watching me?"

"Then why were both goddamn phones busy?"

"Then your not watching me. Some kids were

here. But they've been gone for ten minutes."

"Got the money?"

"Yes."

"Go back on Two Fifty-two to One Forty-four and turn left. Left. Go six miles to Route Sixteen. Left on Sixteen a mile and a quarter. You'll see a two-tone blue Chevy, sixty-one, Jersey plates, parked by an old barn. The trunk key'll be on top of the air cleaner, under the hood. Put the money in the trunk, Feldman, slam it shut, make sure it's shut and check it. Then drop the key through the crack at the top of the window, driver's side. Got it, Feldman? Then go home. And, Feldman, this time we'll be watching you."

"I'll do as you say. Uh, what if I have trouble getting the hood open? I'm not a mechanic."

"You're a smart man. Anybody with your money has got to be smart. You'll get it open."

"And what about the boy?"

"Let's see the money."

"What about the boy?"

"Don't screw around, Feldman." Roy hung up.

26

Harry spotted a parking place and backed the "borrowed" car into it. It wasn't a bad car, a cream-colored Ford hardtop, almost new, low mileage, very ordinary-looking. Ran nice, good tires, a good find. And good plates. Six numbers. Tough to read at a glance. "Now listen, Redhead," he said over the back of the front seat, "you stay under that blanket and out of sight. You hear? You want to queer the whole deal? Stay down. OK?"

"All right already," came a muffled voice.

Harry climbed out of the car and walked around the corner to Hyman's Trading Post, a compact but lushly cluttered pawnshop. The proprietor was haggling with a young musician over a saxophone. The boy had Prince Valiant hair and pimples. Harry walked around the shop, his hands in his pockets, perusing the glittering miscellany dangling from shelves and the ceiling, waiting for the negotiation to end.

"All right, gimme the forty bucks and the hell with you," the boy said.

"I thought you said you planned to come and take it back. The less you get now, the less you pay later."

"I'll be back and the hell with you."

"That's all I'll pay for it, and the hell with you," the little balding proprietor said. He walked over to the register, took out four ten-dollar bills, wrote a ticket and handed them all to the boy. "When do you think you'll be back for this thing?"

"How can I work without a horn?" He took the bills and ticket from the man and stuffed them carelessly into his ragged wallet. "How'd you like to buy an interest in a small group? We make a good sound when we've got horns . . . and we can get work."

The proprietor made a little "leave me out of it" gesture with his hand. "I've got enough heartache trying to own an interest in my own business."

"You oughta have an interest in music. . . . Gimme a break. Help somebody for once. Do something for somebody."

The proprietor studied him for a moment. "You'll use the money to feed some pusher."

"We need the money for expenses, legit expenses," the boy snapped back.

"You I didn't need today. Give me back the ticket."

The boy stared in confusion at the little man's slight smile as he fished out the wallet and then the ticket.

The fragile little shopkeeper scribbled something on the ticket. Then he held the ticket and ballpoint out to the boy. "Here, put your name, address and phone number on here, and let me see your driver's license."

The boy's face lit up. "Mr. Hyman, you're great!" He grabbed the ticket and pen and began writing. "We don't have a phone," he said as he wrote, "but you won't have to call us."

The proprietor looked at the ticket. "Take the instrument."

The boy was exuberant. "Mr. Hyman, I promise you we'll pay off." He grabbed the instrument case and trotted for the door.

"I'll send the police," the proprietor shouted. He turned to Harry, who was walking toward him. "What can I do for you?"

"Uh, I'd like to see something in a target pistol for my boy. Nothing too much. You know, a twenty-two, maybe."

The proprietor walked over to a display case that contained guns and stepped behind it. "May I suggest a Luger? Ten-shot semiautomatic. Shoots twenty-two-caliber long-rifle shells." He lifted a Luger-like pistol out of the case and handed it to Harry.

Harry examined the gun. "Oh, yes, I've heard of these. Looks OK. Give me a box of shells and show me how it loads."

The proprietor pulled a small box of ammunition off a shelf behind him. He took the gun, pressed a release and pulled the magazine from the handle. "You put the bullets right in here and stuff this thing back into the gun."

"Take a couple shells and show me," Harry said.

"Against the rules of the house to load a gun in here. This may be primarily a target pistol, but it's also a very dangerous weapon. You can kill a man with one shot from this gun if it's well aimed."

"Nothing's gonna happen," Harry said, oppressing the mild little man. "I just want to see how it works." He took the magazine, opened the box, took out one shell, pressed it into the magazine and snapped the magazine back into the handle of the gun. "Oh, like that," he said with a smile.

"Please be careful," the proprietor said. "That weapon is loaded and dangerous."

"You mean if I aimed this at your head like I'm doing and pulled the trigger now, it'd scramble your brains?"

The little bald man looked at Harry's expression and fell back against the shelves. "No, please."

"As long as I'm here," Harry said, slipping the cartridges in his pocket, "why don't you just give me all your money?"

The little bald man gradually regained some composure. "Oh, no, not again."

"What do you mean, not again?"

"This is the second time I've been held up in this location. My wife told me not to move here. She's a better businessman than I am." He looked plaintively at Harry. "You wouldn't pull that trigger."

"Not as long as you give me all your money."

The little man walked over to the cash register and opened it with a sigh. "Suppose someone walked in now."

"My line of work, you take chances," Harry answered.

The little man sighed again and began taking money out of the register and placing it in Harry's left palm.

Harry stuffed it in his pocket. There wasn't a lot of it. "Now give me what's in your pockets." He gestured with the gun at the little bald head.

The little proprietor looked at Harry with new respect, the respect one gives a real pro. He very slowly reached in his pocket and pulled out a large roll of bills.

Harry snatched them out of his hand. Then he smiled. "You know, you should've kept that horn. You shouldn't let that kid walk outa here with that forty bucks. That was a mistake."

"That's what you think. That was a good investment."

"How the hell you figure that?"

"At least I have a little chance of getting that money back."

A tiny old lady walked into the shop. Harry pointed the gun at her, and she threw her hands in the air. He motioned her over toward the proprietor and ran out of the shop.

He walked briskly but without running back to the car, got in, started it up and pulled away. The gun was in his belt under his jacket.

"Banner, how'd you do?" the boy shouted. He was out from under the blanket and standing up behind Harry.

"You got your hat on, Redhead?"

The boy reached down and grabbed the hat and dropped it onto his head.

Harry glanced over his shoulder at the boy with the loosely-fitting man's hat resting on his ears.

"I shoulda bought you a nice boy's hat in there. That thing on a head like yours'll attract more attention than that red hair."

"How'd you make out in there? Get some money?

"Here. You count it." He threw the roll and the loose bills over the back of the seat to the boy.

The boy slipped the rubber band off the roll and smoothed the bills out into piles of each denomination. "Just like playing Monopoly," he said.

"Hurry up back there."

"Enough for two houses on Boardwalk and a little left over."

"How much?" Harry said.

"Oh, about four hundred and forty-five dollars. Is that enough to take off on?"

"We need more than that," Harry answered. "We'll have to make another couple stops."

"Can I come with you this time?"

"You just stay down there and covered up, just like I told you. Understand? Else we can't go. Understand?"

"Jesus Christ," the child said. It was the first time he had ever said it, and he said it with a broad grin.

Harry was still reflecting on the child's last line when he spotted a package store that was a perfect setup. It was on a corner with a vacant store next door and nothing across the street. He had to slam on his brakes and back up across the deserted intersection to turn down the street next to the store. He pulled over and parked. "Okay, Redhead. Down under that blanket and stay quiet." He heard the scurrying in the back seat as he climbed out.

The proprietor was alone in the store. He sat at a desk behind the counter and cash register. He had just finished a carry-out dinner on a paper plate and the ruins from it were scattered about the desktop. He was picking his teeth.

"I hate to disturb you," Harry said as he walked in.

"Quite all right," the man answered. He dropped the toothpick and jumped up. He brushed his palms on the sides of his pants. "Just having my supper. Can I help you with anything?"

"I won't be a minute," Harry said. "Just a quick stop." He paused for a moment in front of the bourbons and lifted off one bottle of a very expensive brand. "Maybe I'll take one of these." He walked over to the counter.

"Very good, sir. What else can I help you with?"

Harry put the bottle down and looked at the man. He was obviously only a clerk. He couldn't possibly own or run anything. He was thin, with straight hair slicked straight back, gold showing in his teeth, the familiar old "yessir" look in his eyes. "Quick, now," Harry said, "give me all of your money." He slipped the Luger from his belt and aimed it point-blank at the clerk's face.

The clerk threw his hands in the air. "Please

don't shoot." His face was a masterpiece of total fright.

"Put your hands down and get that drawer open and be quick about it."

The clerk fumbled with the drawer and the money, pouring it out on the counter.

"Never mind the change," Harry snapped.

"Yessir, yessir," the clerk answered, ignoring the change on the counter.

"Now, give me *your* money and be quick." Harry held the gun closer to his head.

"Yessir, yessir, yessir. Just don't shoot. Please don't shoot." He pulled out his wallet and lifted out five ten-dollar bills. "I got paid today." He was shaking and his face was wet.

Harry grabbed all the bills and stuffed them in his pocket. "Got any more money anywhere around here?" Once again, he held the gun up to the clerk's head.

"Please! Honest. No. Please!" The clerk was plaintive, almost crying. Then the clerk suddenly looked at the front door as though someone were about to walk in.

Harry heard the door open and dropped sideways so that he could cover both the door and the clerk. He looked in the direction of the door. It was Gary, grinning from ear to ear, the big hat circling down over his ears. "I thought I told you to stay put!" Harry shouted.

"I wanted to see how you do it," the child answered with his grin.

Harry turned back to the clerk. "Don't you do anything for at least thirty minutes. Is that clear?"

"Yessir, yessir."

"Because if you do, I'm going to come back and put a bullet in your head. Is that clear?"

"Yessir, yessir."

"All right." Harry started backing out of the store. "If I was you, I'd play it smart and do as I say." He stopped. "Almost forgot something." He stepped quickly forward and grabbed his fifth of whiskey with his left hand. Then he hurried out with the child following at his heels. When he got back to the car, he glanced in through the car window, and all the money from the pawnshop was still spread out in neat piles on the back seat. It was clearly visible from the sidewalk. He laughed aloud and climbed in. The child got in from the door on the sidewalk side and climbed over into the back seat.

"How'd we do this time, Banner? How much did you get?"

"I don't know. Here, you count it." He threw the money over to the child, throwing it casually, like scrap paper. He listened to the child count the money.

"Three hundred and eighty-eight dollars," the child said in a most assumed manner.

"Now put it together with the other and count it all and see how much we got."

"Three eighty-eight and four forty-five adds up to . . . umm . . . eight thirty-three. That's enough for four houses on Boardwalk and thirty-three dollars left over."

"You figure that in your head? How do you know you're right?"

"Mr. Goldschmidt says I have an eighth-grade aptitude in mathematics."

Harry smiled and shook his head.

"Think that man in the store will do nothing for thirty minutes the way you told him?"

Harry laughed. "He'll still be standing there shaking this time tomorrow."

"Banner?" The child paused, in thought. "Would you have shot him if he wouldn't give you the money?" He asked the question slowly, in a searching voice.

"You don't have to shoot 'em, Redhead. Just tell him you might and they do what you say."

"I know, but would you have?"

"Nah, I just scare 'em a little."

"Did you ever shoot anybody?"

"Course not. Never had to."

"I know, but would you, if you had to?"

"Course not, Redhead. You don't have to. You just have to scare 'em good. People don't argue with a gun."

"Have we got enough money yet, Banner?"

Harry remained quiet for a moment as he drove. Then he stopped in the middle of an intersection and abruptly turned left. "We'll never stack up enough on these little jobs," he said, speaking to himself. "We're going where we know there's enough. Yessir. We're going to the well. Where there's a bucketful waiting for us."

"Where are we going now, Banner?"

"To get the money we need."

"I know, but where's that?"

"Listen, Redhead. Take all that money back

there and stack it in one stack. Roll it up and put that rubber band around it and hand it to me."

The child was silent for a moment as he followed the instructions. He handed Harry the roll. "Where are we going to get the rest of the money, Banner?"

"Now listen, Redhead. You want to go with me, don't you? Now you're going to have to be a tough little kid if you do. You're going to have to sit alone in the dark for a few minutes and wait for me. Everything depends on it. You're going to have to sit alone in the dark and not get scared. Can you do it?"

"I—I don't know. I'm afraid of the dark."

"It'll only be for a few minutes, Redhead. You gotta do it. There'll be some lights way off in the distance you can look at."

"Where are you going to get the money?" The child climbed over into the front seat and sat next to Harry.

Harry drove on for a while without answering. It was a cloudy night, slightly windy, with rapidly moving cloud formations and rapidly changing shades of darkness. The child seemed relaxed while they were driving through areas that were built up, but he became nervous and apprehensive on prolonged stretches that were empty and unlit. Harry finally stopped the car on a deserted road. "You see up there ahead? There's some lights. You just sit here and look at those lights. Just sit right here and I'll only be gone a few minutes."

"Banner . . . I'm scared." The child's voice was tiny, hardly audible.

"Here, listen to the radio. And look at those lights. I'll only be gone a few minutes, and when I get back, we'll be on our way." He could see terror in the child's wide eyes in the reflected light from the radio. He could almost smell fear about the child, who was beginning to wheeze slightly. He gave the child's shoulder a little squeeze. "C'mon, Redhead. I'll be right back." He climbed out of the car and walked off into the darkness behind the car.

27

Harry walked up the driveway to the house, taking quick steps but staying out of a strip of light that cut across the driveway from between a pair of cracked curtains. The garage doors were open and the light was on. He stepped inside. The keys were in the car. The radio or TV upstairs was being played at high volume. He thought about the basement stairs but decided against them. It wouldn't be easy getting up those without being heard.

He went back outside and tiptoed up the stone steps to the front yard. He walked up on the stoop and looked in through the little windows in the front door. Roy was not in the living room. He stepped down to the yard and around to the side windows. Roy was in the kitchen pouring a drink. He walked back around to the front stoop and tried the door.

When Roy walked back into the living room, Harry was standing there with the Luger pointed at him. Roy dropped the glass from surprise. "Harry! What the hell are you up to?"

"Gimme half the money."

"Harry, where's the kid?"

"Gimme half the money."

"Harry, you're outa your head. That kid'll be the end of you."

"Gimme half the money. This'll be a good place to split up."

"Harry, let's get rid of the kid. Everything came off perfect. Nobody knows nothing. We'll be free. The kid's the only one who knows us."

"Gimme half the money. I'm not asking for all of it. Just half. That's my share. Now, where is it?"

"Harry, what are you pointing a gun at me for? We're partners." Roy twisted his lips into an ugly smile. "You wouldn't shoot me. You never shot anybody and you never will." He began walking forward. "You're just a nice, big, soft, easy-going nickel and dime . . ."

Harry aimed at the floor and pulled the trigger. The little crack of the .22 startled Roy, who stopped and stepped back.

"Hey, what kinda little popgun you got there, Harry? Little BB gun? You can't stop anybody with that thing."

"Roy, don't monkey around. Just gimme half the money."

"Where'd you get that gun, Harry?"

"In a pawnshop. It shoots ten times, and the slugs'll hurt. Now where's the money?"

Roy hesitated. Then he half laughed. "When

you invited me to do this job with you, I never thought you'd run off with the kid instead of me."

"You still have your half of the take, and you're free to go anywhere you want. Just give me my half."

"The money's in the bedroom." Roy said it and stood still, staring at Harry.

"Then let's go in there. You first and slow."

They walked slowly into the bedroom, Harry keeping the gun aimed point-blank at the middle of Roy's back. Roy walked over to the desk which held a partly opened brown paper package.

"Divide it into two equal piles, Roy. Then get over there, outa the way."

Roy divided it and stepped away from it. Harry walked over and with his left hand began stuffing one pile into his jacket pockets. He filled one of the side pockets and one inside pocket. Then he paused, watching Roy intently. He stuffed a bundle into his pants pocket and paused again.

"More'n you got pockets for, ain't it, Harry? . . . You're doing this wrong, pal. This ain't your best chance. Your best chance is my way. And if I catch up to you and that kid, I'll still kill the kid. And you, too, if I have to."

Harry continued watching Roy. He carefully transferred the gun to his left hand and with his right hand stuffed a bundle of money into his right-side pocket. He took another bundle and moved it toward his left inside jacket pocket. He fumbled for the pocket, finally looking down into his jacket. Roy rushed at him. He aimed at Roy and pulled the trigger, but the empty gun only clicked. As Roy's shoulder hit him in the stomach, he slashed at Roy's head with the gun barrel with all his strength. They went down, and Roy landed on top of him but rolled off to the side, clutching his head. Harry scrambled up, took the gun by the barrel and hit Roy viciously with the butt. Roy humped and sank.

Harry dropped the gun and turned Roy over with both hands. Roy's face was bloody, but he was breathing more or less evenly. "I was wondering how I was going to walk away from you, Roy," he muttered to the silent form. "Thanks for your help." He grabbed the one remaining bundle of money from his half and ran from the room. He ran by the phone in the hall, stopped, thought about yanking the wire from the wall. Deciding against it, he went down the steps into the basement. He got into the car, backed it out of the garage and drove the few hundred yards back to the car where he had left the child. He jumped out and into the other car. "Let's go, Redhead. Redhead?"

The child was gone.

28

Harry got back out of the car. "Redhead? Redhead? Gary?" He called in a normal voice at first, then louder. He walked around the car, staring into the dark woods. "Redhead? Gary?" He leaned back against the car and massaged himself on his neck. *"Redhead? Gary? Redhead?"* He was shouting at the top of his voice. He stopped and waited but heard no answer. He shouted again and waited. Nothing.

He stared up the road in the direction of the lights. If the kid had run, he would run toward the lights. There was a streetlight several hundred yards up the road at an intersection. A few hundred more yards up the road there were two or three houses with lights on.

He got back into the car he had stolen. It was hot, but not as hot as Roy's car which had been used for the drop. He flung the keys to Roy's car into the underbrush off the road. As he started moving forward, he began to make out a small figure under the streetlight. It was the child, wearing the big hat and crying convulsively.

Harry accelerated and then slammed to a stop in front of the boy and jumped out. "Redhead!"

The child was hysterical. "Banner! I got frightened!" He rushed to Harry, who was kneeling, and threw his arms around him. "I was frightened," he sobbed.

"It's OK now, pal. We got the money just like I promised, and we're on our way. It's OK now. We're all set."

The child gradually slowed down his sobbing to an occasional shudder as they began driving. He was wheezing heavily.

"You'd better settle down a little bit and use some of your medicine," Harry said in a quiet voice.

The child choked up again. "I don't have any more. It's all used up." He began to cry. "I used it up back there."

"It's OK. It's OK," Harry said in a soothing voice. "All we have to do is stop and get you some more."

29

Harry drove for a while with the child at his side, huddled close to him. The child had stopped crying and was resting quietly, but his breathing was noisy. Harry needed an out-of-the-way drugstore to pick up the child's medicine. He wondered how completely the cops had covered the drugstores. Something else to have to sweat. But the kid needed the stuff. Jesus, what wheezing! Then he thought about the money. Pockets bulging with twenty-five big ones. Jesus, that's a lot of money! But not enough. Not enough for that one big payday. That one big payday to end all paydays. Nowhere near enough.

"Tell me some more about where we're going to go, Banner."

"Everywhere, Redhead. Anywhere you want to go. . . . All over the country, lots of places."

"I know, but name some of the places. Texas?"

"Texas."

"Grand Coulee?"

"Gotta think, now, Redhead. We'll talk about it later. Lemme think now."

The child got quiet.

Harry thought about taking the kid all over the world. He thought about wiring the kid's parents and telling them not to worry. The kid was in good hands. Their money was being well spent. The kid was safe and having a great time. It was the best thing that ever happened to him.

But then his thoughts returned to the business at hand. He had to get organized. He had to think of the things he needed to get started. He had to get the money out of his pockets. You just don't walk around with money bulging out of your pockets. . . .

Harry spotted a drugstore which didn't look crowded. "C'mon, Redhead, we'll get your medicine there." He pulled over to the curb in front of the drugstore. "Here, let's put this money in the glove compartment while I go in there." He began pulling bundles of bills from all pockets.

The boy perked up at the sight of all the money and watched in fascination as neatly taped blocks of bills seemed to be emerging from everywhere . . . Monoply money, but more of it, and real.

Harry began cleaning the glove compartment. Countless bits of paper, pliers, two screwdrivers, napkins, a flashlight, chrome polish. He considered throwing the miscellany into the street and then dropped it onto the floor behind the front seat. He began stuffing the bills into the empty compartment. He took the roll of bills with the rubber band, peeled off a few of them, folded them and put them in his pants pocket. Then he flattened out the rest, slipped the rubber band around them and stuffed them in with the big bundles. "Now give me the bottle from your medicine, Redhead, and stay down out of sight." He gave the boy's head a playful rub through the big hat. "And keep the hat on."

"But I don't have the bottle anymore. I threw it away when it was empty."

"How can I get you any more?"

"I know the name of it."

"Then tell me the name of it."

"It's called Asma-neft Solution A-four."

Harry repeated it over and over as he got out and went into the store. There was only one attendant, the pharmacist. He was scooping ice-cream cones for two young teen-age girls. A woman customer was also waiting for him.

"I believe you were here first," he said to the woman after he had finished with the ice cream and made change.

"I would like some of this shampoo, but I don't know which type to take. It comes for three kinds of hair. My sister uses it and says I should try it. My sister lives in Philadelphia and she visited last weekend and said I should try it, but I don't know which one. I live across in the Parkview."

Harry fidgeted nervously, waiting for the exchange to end.

"Do you have oily hair?" the pharmacist asked.

"Certainly not," she snapped.

"Well, do you have dry hair?"

"I don't think so. At least I never thought of

it as dry hair. What would you say I had?"

"Why don't you try the one for regular hair?" the pharmacist asked. "They're really not that different. It should work fine."

"Maybe so." She picked up each of the three bottles and studied the labels while the pharmacist stood politely quiet. "I think I'll take the one for oily hair," she said, finally, with a "please keep your reactions to yourself" inflection in her voice.

"Surely." The pharmacist put the bottle in a bag and made change. "I'm sure you'll be pleased with it." He turned to Harry as the lady walked out.

"I hope she gets it clean," Harry said.

"She bought the right one, I think," the pharmacist answered, smiling. "What would you like?"

"I'd like some Asmaneft A-four Solution, something like that. It's the stuff kids use from these little plastic things and inhale when they have asthma. Comes in a little thing like this." He held his thumb and forefinger to indicate size. "My, uh, niece. She's visiting the wife and I. She ran out. Didn't bring enough."

"Oh?" the pharmacist said, and he lifted one eyebrow and then looked up at Harry, and their eyes locked for a terrifying eternity of an instant. Then the pharmacist glanced toward the door. "I think I have some of that on hand," he said, slowly, as though uncertain about what to do. He hesitated and then backed up toward a shelf, turned and took something off.

"I'll take all you have." Harry felt sickened.

He felt his face get hot as the druggist returned and began studying him.

"I have three bottles on hand, two twenty-five each," he said without taking his eyes off Harry.

Harry pulled out the folded bills and handed him a ten. He watched the pharmacist studying him, noting clothes, features, hair, everything, while moving back to the register to make change. Harry concentrated on trying to relax, to appear at ease.

"Anything else?" the pharmacist asked.

"That'll be all, thanks," Harry answered. He took the bottles and the change and started for the door. The pharmacist followed him. Harry gave him a questioning look and then walked out. The pharmacist followed him out and stopped in the doorway. Harry walked to the car and got in. He glanced at the pharmacist, and their eyes met for another instant. The pharmacist was studying the car.

As Harry closed the door, the child bobbed up, hat and all. "Get down!" Harry snapped. He dropped the three tiny boxes on the seat. Then he started the car and pulled away. "There's the medicine. Put it in your pocket and don't lose it. It was expensive!"

The child looked up at Harry's intense expression and didn't speak.

Harry rubbed himself on the back of the neck. "I gotta think," he said. "I gotta think. I gotta think."

30

Four cars, all four-door sedans, moved in silent, unobtrusive caravan along the brightly lit main street, stopping for lights, observing the posted speed limit of 45 mph. Each car contained four men in business suits, who talked quietly among themselves. The cars turned off onto a side street and continued in line, moving briskly but not racing. They continued for about two miles and then turned again, the small, modest homes thinning out as they went.

As they passed the end of a row of houses and the street became desolate, the lead car pulled over and stopped. The other pulled up behind it and also stopped, cutting lights and motors. Lights popped on in the cars as doors opened, the men climbing out into the darkness. They began unloading gear from the trunks of the four cars. Then, carrying the gear, they assembled and held a quiet discussion, one of them leading the discussion, pointing farther down the dark road toward an area grown over with tall, closely spaced trees and underbrush. He gave instructions in terse monotone, making gestures with his hands.

The group discussion broke up and the men started down the road on foot, carrying the miscellaneous equipment. Some three hundred yards down the road they approached a small plain house with lights burning inside. The party of men began to disperse and, staying fifty to seventy-five yards from the house, to encircle it. A group of five men stood by the mailbox near the mouth of the driveway and contemplated the house, pointing at various windows and other details and speaking in whispers, while the rest of the men, in twos and threes, positioned themselves at various angles around the house.

All the men remained inactive for fifteen or twenty minutes, watching the house intently for any sign of activity. One of the group near the mailbox held a flashlight to its side and turned it on for a second, just long enough to read the name. Esposito. The mailbox group continued to maintain quiet, still watching for a sign of life from the house.

Finally, one of the men lifted a bullhorn and pressed the button, but before he could speak into it, another of the men reached up and touched the horn, and the man holding it released the button and dropped it down from his mouth. Then the man who had touched the horn motioned to two of the others and pointed at the house.

The two men started walking up the driveway but, hearing their footsteps on the gravel, stepped off onto the grass. As they approached the house, they pulled revolvers from inside their jackets. They moved up flush against the house and waited for several minutes for sound in the house. Hearing nothing, one of them eased his head up and glanced into the living-room window. Seeing no activity, he glanced at the other windows on the front of the house, which were too high to look into, and motioned to the other man with him to follow him. They moved around the corner to the end of the house, glanced in the kitchen window, then the kitchen door, then moved to the rear of the house, where once again the windows were too high. The windows at the other end of the house were above the garage doors and even farther out of reach.

The two men came back to the front of the house and moved across the yard, back to the mailbox. After some conversation, the two men and one more put on gas masks and started back toward the house, the extra man carrying a tear-gas gun. The first of the men, holding his revolver, tiptoed up the steps to the front door and looked through one of the three small windows in the door. He tried the door and, finding it unlocked, opened it quietly and entered, gun first, motioning to the other two to follow. They stepped across the living room, glanced into the kitchen and then were starting down the hall toward the bedrooms when they saw Roy on the floor. They moved slowly down the hall, guns first, toward Roy, checking every door on the way—the other bedrooms, the bathroom, a closet, the cellar stairs and cellar—turning on all lights as they went.

They stood over Roy and peeled off their gas masks. A target pistol lay a few feet away. One of the men kneeled and turned Roy's head to see the injury. He wiped his fingers on Roy's shirt and then felt Roy's wrist. One of the other men walked over to the desk, picked up a bundle of money, put it back down and then, glancing at Roy and the others, walked to the front door. Standing framed in the light of the door, he motioned to the two men remaining by the mailbox, who jumped up into the yard and moved quickly toward the house.

The five men clustered around Roy, two kneeling, checking him for his injury and the contents of his pockets, the other three standing. One of those standing went back outside. Another went back into the hall to the phone and began placing a call. The third went into the bathroom and grabbed the single soiled towel hanging there, threw it into the basin and ran cold water on it. He lifted out the dripping towel and carried it into the bedroom. Kneeling next to Roy, he laid it on his blood-caked face. Roy stirred. He picked the towel back up and twisted it so that a stream of cool water fell on Roy's face. Roy began to roll his head from side to side and sputter, finally mouthing a stream of garbled profanity.

"Nice to see you again, Walls," Schamper said. "Where's the child?"

"Child? What child?" Roy sat up, cursing the pain in his head.

31

Harry was driving faster. "It's gonna be touch and go now, Redhead," he said.

The child was on his knees on the front seat, watching the surroundings go by. "What does that mean?"

"That means we gotta be cool. And everything's got to go just right. We gotta be real cool."

"What are you going to do now, Banner?" The child was excited. It was the first real excitement he had ever experienced.

"We gotta get a couple things. But that's OK. We'll be going where they least expect us to go, at least for the time being. You gotta stay covered up when I tell you to."

"What are you going to get?"

"For one thing, I'm gonna get you a decent hat. What kind do you want?"

"I want a surfer's hat."

"What the hell's a surfer's hat?"

"It's all cloth, and it has a brim all the way

around like this one, only it's all cloth. And they're all different colors."

"If they got 'em where we're going, I'll get a surfer's hat. Now, another thing, Redhead." He hesitated. "If I get in a jam and do something crazy that you don't understand, well, whatever it is, don't worry about it. Just do as I say. Just go along with it. Can you remember that?"

"Like if you do what? I don't understand."

"Well, I don't know exactly myself. Depends what we run into."

"What will you do?"

"Well, suppose I act like I'm going to do something you know I wouldn't do. Like to you. Just go along with it. Understand? Act scared. Just don't be scared. But act scared. OK?"

The child looked up at him. He didn't understand.

"Well, you know I wouldn't do anything to you, Redhead."

"Yeah, but, what are you going to do?"

Harry slowed down. "This is where we want to go. Now duck down and cover up again." He had pulled to a stop in the middle of the street, waiting for traffic to allow him to make a left turn into the entrance to a discount store parking lot. The parking area was largely obscured from the road, and the entry was long and single lane. The child scrambled over into the back as he pulled in. "Remember what I told you, Redhead." He eased into a parking place. "Stay down now."

He got out and went into the store. It was

Saturday night, and the store was bustling. All check-out lanes were in use, and there were lines at each. People were pushing carts containing their children and their purchases, things ranging from clothing to garden tools to appliances, TV antennas, motor oil. Harry grabbed a cart and moved quickly around the store. He picked up two small pieces of luggage and a small cloth hat he hoped was a surfer's hat. He went to the cosmetics area and pulled a package down he hoped would dye the child's hair dark. There were a dozen preparations that looked almost as if they might work. The labels were hopelessly confusing.

He moved quickly to a check-out line. The wait seemed endless as the two young girls operated the register and packed the bags, stapling each bag shut with the register tape. Twice while he waited, the girl on the register couldn't make out a price and rang a little bell and a brisk young man, very businesslike despite his pimpled face, came over to give assistance. Harry finally reached the register.

"I can't tell if this price is eight seventy-six or nine seventy-six," the girl on the register said as she squinted at a smudgy number on a string tag on one of the small suitcases.

"It's nine seventy-six," Harry said.

She looked at him. "OK. If you say so."

"Do you want these suitcases in bags?" asked the other girl. "We have these big paper bags."

"Not necessary," Harry answered.

"We can't wrap them," she said.

"I'll take them as they are. I'm in a hurry."

The girl took a squirt of paper tape with the store's name on it and stuck it to itself around the handle. "This'll show that you paid for it."

Harry paid the total and left. The old cop assigned to the door of the store looked totally bored, an old badge who was not good for much any more but spending a Saturday night as a super, covering the door of a discount store. The one big crowd of the week. Saturday night shopping at the local discount store. It called for a cop, any cop. It gave the old man a payday and a chance to air his uniform.

Harry hurried back to the car. He glanced into the next car. The keys were in it. It was a red and white station wagon. He opened the door to it and threw the luggage and package on the back seat. Then he opened the door to the car containing the child. "Redhead, we just bought a new car. Let's go. And bring the blanket."

The child jumped up and scrambled onto the floor of the back seat of the station wagon. Harry climbed in, started the car and headed for the parking lot exit. He did not see a man waving at him, running after him. He did not hear the man's shouts. He did not see the man go running back to the old cop, shouting and pointing after him after he had disappeared from the parking lot.

32

Harry was driving fast. "I hope somebody had a lot of things to buy, Redhead," he said. "Check the hat in the bag back there. That a surfer's hat?"

The child pulled the hat out of the bag. "Hey, Banner, this is neat!" He pulled it on and climbed over into the front seat. "Man!" he sensed real excitement and was caught up in it.

"We're on our way now, Redhead."

The child was on his knees, watching the sights again. He was a kid on a trip, going somewhere. "Are we heading for the airport now?"

"We're on our way to the airport. And they're all out watching for the car that's parked in that parking lot back there."

The child suddenly whirled around and looked at Harry. "Banner!"

Harry glanced at him. "What's the matter now?"

"The money!"

Harry slammed on the brakes. He threw an arm out to catch the child and keep him from crashing into the dashboard. He made a U-turn and started back, driving even faster. "I hope some man had a lot to buy," he said again, to himself. "Don't forget what I told you," he said to the child. "About doing something crazy, I mean."

The child didn't answer because he still didn't understand.

Harry got back to the store's parking lot about ten to fifteen minutes after he had left. He had to wait again for the turn into the entrance. He started down the long one-lane entry road, and when the full lot came into view, there was a police car standing near where the other car was parked. He stopped. A car behind him almost bumped into him. He turned and waved to the car behind him to let him out. But there was another car behind that one. Both cars blew their horns.

He just sat for a moment. He massaged himself on the back of the neck. He rubbed his hand across his wet forehead. He was trembling. He finally started up and headed for the middle of the crowd around the police car. The owner of the station wagon spotted him and began excitedly pointing at him. The two young policemen from the patrol car drew their guns and crouched. The old policeman stepped behind the patrol car. The spectators, seeing the drawn guns, scattered and jumped behind cars. Some broke into a dead run away from the scene. Some watched from behind cars. Most crouched completely out of sight.

Harry pulled up within less than a hundred feet of the policemen. He reached over, opened the door on the child's side and pushed him out. Then he slid across and stepped out behind him. He held the child's left upper arm tightly with his left hand and kept his right hand behind the child. He crouched slightly and started moving forward.

When he came within forty feet of the two policemen, he gave the child's arm a menacing jerk and shouted, "Stay clear and let us by or I'll blow this child's brains out!"

The two policemen looked dumbfounded. Then one shouted, "He's got the Feldman kid!"

The child looked at the policemen and turned and looked back up at Harry with a totally confused expression. "Banner?" Then a sudden look of realization swept across his face. For a moment he smiled a tiny silly smile. He tried to get the smile off his face and bring back a frightened look. He tried hard. But despite all his concentration, the silly smile was winning out over the mock fright.

The two policemen began to move apart, a step at a time, in a gesture of encirclement, stalking. "Don't do it!" Harry snapped. "Stand still! Real still!" The policemen stopped moving, stiffened and then stood motionless. Harry gave the child another menacing jerk, and the child's half-smile faded but then began to creep back. "Put your guns away and button 'em up tight. Let's go! Do it!" The boy's smile broadened slightly as he watched the policemen do as they were told.

Harry continued moving slowly toward the car with the money in it, keeping the boy between himself and the two policemen, keeping his right hand behind the boy, his left hand throttling the boy's left upper arm. "Come after me and I'll kill this child. Understand? I got nothing to lose. Understand? Nothing!" He made his way with the child to the driver's side of the car, the side away from the policemen. "So don't push me. Understand? Or I'll splatter this kid's head and you can say you made me do it. OK?" The two young cops remained motionless.

With quick jerky movements, Harry released the child's arm, yanked open the car door, shoved the child inside, seated himself behind the wheel and slammed the door. The key was there where he had left it. He started the car with a roar and lunged for the parking-lot exit. The two cops headed for their car, climbed in and got on their radio.

Harry drove quickly about six blocks from the store along the main street and then turned off onto a sparsely built-up side street, where he drove slowly, naturally, unobtrusively. He began taking deep controlled breaths, struggling to regain his composure.

"Hey, Banner, the money's still here." The child was rummaging among the packets of bills in the lighted glove compartment.

"You did all right back there in the parking lot, Redhead. All right."

"Let's go to California. Are we on our way now?"

Harry wiped his face on his upper jacket sleeves, first one side, then the other. He made turn after turn, driving slowly around the dimly lit residential area. "I did pretty well myself," he reflected aloud. "Considering I didn't even have a gun. Pretty well."

"Are we on our way, now, Banner?"

Harry pulled the car over on a stretch of totally deserted road, cut the lights, then the engine. He wiped his face on his sleeves again and then sought the comfort of a hand on the back of his neck.

"Banner. What'd you stop for?"

Harry remained quiet.

"Banner. What'd you stop here for? It's pitch black out here." His voice was getting smaller.

Harry reached over into the glove compartment and began taking the bundles of money and stuffing them into his jacket pockets.

"Banner?"

"We'll never make it tonight, Redhead."

"Aren't we going to California?"

"Not tonight, Redhead. We won't make it. We lost our suitcases and your hat. We'll need to trade cars again, and we could have trouble. It's getting late. It's getting late for the last flight. It's no use, Redhead. We'll have to give it up for tonight."

"Aren't we going to California?"

"Not tonight."

"What are we going to do?"

"I'm sending you home."

"I thought we were going to California."

Without answering, Harry started the motor, turned on the lights and eased away from the side of the road.

"Banner, aren't we going to California like you said?"

"Another time, maybe, Redhead. But not to-night. . . . But don't give up hope. It's still a good idea."

"But if I go back home, how can we go to California?"

"I'll come and pick you up and we'll go."

"Yeah. Fat chance." The child slumped against the seat, and his eyes began to tear up as they drove on in silence.

Harry drove for about fifteen minutes, slowly, over dark residential streets. He finally came back to a main road. A few yards to the right of the intersection stood a diner. He turned the car to the right and pulled to a stop, off the road, some fifty yards past the diner, which was lit up but not busy. "Redhead, walk back to that diner back there and tell them to call your father to come and get you. But don't tell them anything about me. OK? Don't tell anyone anything about me. Not my name, not what I look like, what we did, where we went, nothing. Especially don't tell them where we had plans to go to. Will you do that?"

"Then we're not going to California?" The boy's eyes were wet, but he was maintaining control of himself.

"No point in trying it now if we're going to get stopped. Things are just too hot. If we try it now, we're dead ducks. But if we do everything right, we might be able to make it. Don't give up the idea. Just keep it a secret. If you do everything I tell you to do, we may get to go."

"What do you want me to do?"

"Right now, I want you to go to that diner after I leave, call home, and then don't tell nobody nothing about anything that's happened since we picked you up. Nobody nothing. OK? Here's a dollar for the phone. They'll change it for you in there."

The child looked up at Harry through a shimmering wall of water. He started to say something else but then choked on it.

"Hey, wait a minute, Redhead. I just remembered. I got something for you." Harry began fumbling in his pants pocket. "It's right here somewhere. Something special. I made it for you. Myself. Took a lot of work." He finally located it and brought it out of his pocket and handed it to the boy.

The child sniffled as he took it. "What is it?"

"What is it? Whadda ya mean, what is it? What does it look like?"

"I don't know."

"Well, look at it."

The boy examined it more closely in the dim light. "I don't know. It looks like a little piece of wood."

"Is that all it looks like?"

"What's it supposed to look like?"

"An owl."

"This is an owl?"

"Sure. Don't you see the pointed ears? And the big eyes? Jesus, I put quite a few hours into that. It woulda been better, but the wood was too hard. I made it special for you."

"It's very nice. Thank you." These two things must be said on accepting all gifts. But it was clearly nothing special. Not at this moment.

"You better go, Redhead. Remember. Don't tell nobody nothing. We may still get to go if you keep everything secret. But we can't make it now. Understand?" Harry reached over the child's lap and opened the car door. He watched the child climb out and slowly push it closed. It didn't close all the way, so Harry reached over and, with a quick snap, opened it a crack and slammed it shut. "Don't give up hope, Redhead," he said through the open window. Then he pulled away.

"Yeah, Redhead, don't give up hope," Harry mouthed to himself after he had driven away. "Just keep hoping and keep your mouth shut." Coulda been a good idea. Take the kid a million miles away and get some more money for him. Coulda been. Just didn't quite work out. Didn't quite work out. Mighta worked as a surprise, maybe. Complete surprise. But, Jesus, not now. Not with every cop in the state organized. Be lucky to save my ass as it is. Gotta disappear from the face of the earth and come back somebody else. Harry Banner is a dead man. Twenty-five's not a fair price for that. Ought to be more. Lot more. . . .

The small boy shuddered a time or two as he watched Banner's car disappear. Then he sat down on the curb and contemplated the tiny wooden block in the dim light. An owl? His nasal passages began to constrict, forcing him to open his mouth to breathe, and the air faintly whistled as it flowed in and out. Finally, his face wet and his wheeze getting worse, he got up and walked toward the diner. When he reached the steps, he paused, stood the little wooden block on the top step, next to one of the rusted black steel posts supporting the hand railing. Then he walked up the four steps and went inside.

33

"Come in, June. Sit down."

She felt sickened as she walked toward his
smile. She knew the smile well. She had seen it
often in her role as his secretary. It was only a
trace of a smile, nearer a smirk. It stated with
certainty that he held all the cards and in the
interests of expedience he was going to be forced
to play them efficiently. It wasn't always pleasant
playing them that way, the smile said, but it
was the way things had to be. Being a winner
entails a certain responsibility, a seriousness of
purpose, a dedication to consistency, a pledge to
always expending that little extra push at the cost
of whatever personal loss might be involved. She
had studied the smile many times while present
to witness, or notarize, or record a transaction in-
volving one of his business adversaries. It always
took a little something out of her. He seldom lost.
In fact, he seldom broke even. But this time the
smile was a little different. It was the first time she

had ever seen the unmistakable smile when he was looking at *her*. She felt weak.

She had brought her pad and pencil with her. Of course, it was clumsy, but why not pretend it was just another Monday morning? She sat down and primly crossed her legs. "Are things settling down and getting back to normal at home?" It came out awkwardly, almost as if she were a cub reporter and he a stranger. It was an unnerving sensation to feel all at once so completely foreign in *her* chair opposite his desk.

"Have you heard from your brother?" he said through a smile.

"Oh, for God's sake, Victor." She looked away. She couldn't look at him. Then she added, still not looking at him, "Really, Victor, don't you think three hours of police interrogation yesterday was enough?"

"You two had gotten very close. I would expect you to be the first person . . . probably the only person he would contact."

"Victor, how is Gary?" The awkward feeling was gone. But he was suddenly a new entity, a new quantity. The sensation was one of something coming to an end with crashing abruptness.

"And I doubt if you'd let anyone know if he did. Am I right?" He continued to smile.

"Victor, how is Gary?" She said it with a quickened inflection, trying to indicate the subject should be changed.

"You know, kidnapping is a federal offense, June, dear. Even after the kidnapped party is safely back. Your brother is still guilty of kid-

202

napping. And aiding, or harboring, or even with-
holding information on a fugitive guilty of a federal offense is a serious offense in itself. Have you
considered the implications. . . ."

"Victor, stop it! He won't contact me. And
should he, I'll insist he turn himself in."

"I'm sure you will." His smile broadened slightly.
"How is Gary? How has he taken the whole
thing?"

"Gary is in the hospital."

"Oh, God! What for?"

"George Berman wasn't able to get him quieted
down yesterday. The boy's had quite a trauma.
George felt the best way to handle things was to
put him in for a couple of days until he begins
to settle down."

"I'm sure he'll be all right. Kids get over things
quickly. Harry may have kidnapped him for
money, but I know Harry pretty well, and I'm sure
he wouldn't harm him or even be unkind to him."

"I think you're very wrong. Gary was so shaken
up, so frightened by your brother, he wouldn't
tell us anything about him. Even after he had been
assured we knew about him." Feldman's smile
still persisted. "I don't know quite what your gentle
brother did to that child during the couple of
days he had him, but whatever it was, it sure put
the fear of God into him."

"Well, the important thing, Victor, is that the
whole thing is over with. One of them is locked
up and . . . I'm sure they'll catch Harry in due
time. Funny, I never liked Roy Walls from the
things Harry used to say about him. I don't know

what it was, but I never felt right about him, somehow, even though I'd never laid eyes on him until last night on the news." She looked back at Feldman. She had been staring off into space while rambling about Roy Walls, and as her eyes met Feldman's again, she found him studying her and smiling, the smile more intense, as though he were preparing to stipulate a set of surrender terms. She returned his stare without speaking for several seconds until finally she began to wither under its pressure. She was no match. "Victor, what is it?"

"I think you know what I have to do. Really, I feel I have no choice. I'm sure you understand, at least you will after you think about it."

"Victor, what on earth are you talking about?" The color drained from her face, and she began to tremble.

"You know, the police said it had to be an inside job. Of course, I don't always think the police are right about everything. You know I've never been one to give unqualified support to any police agencies. You've heard me many times voice this particular stand." He spoke at a slow, step-by-step, thought-by-thought pace, watching her intently for the effect his line of discussion was having. "But under the circumstances, you see, the fact that he was your brother and you saw him regularly and you were so familiar with, in fact, helped plan everything that went on within my household," he paused, as if wondering where to penetrate with the next thrust to keep the pain minimal, "well, I'm sure you can understand the

kind of social and public"—he paused again, and
his expression changed ever so slightly to reveal
a suddenly remembered something—"and private
pressure that I'm under. You know, of course, that
I don't personally—"

"Victor," she interrupted, "for God's sake, what
is it? Get to the point."

He tried to make his smile reflect warmth.
"June, please try to be understanding of the
circumstances. I think you can appreciate that I
would be subject to considerable criticism, in
fact, scandal, yes, at least scandal, if you were
to continue in the position of my private secretary,
regardless of how things actually were."

"Victor, do you believe for one minute that I
had anything whatever to do with this whole
thing?"

"Please, June, try to understand that it isn't
what I believe."

"Answer my question. Do you think I so much
as had any prior knowledge, any inkling, that my
brother Harry was up to anything like this?"

"What I believe has nothing to do with it."

"It has everything to do with it."

"Please. It isn't necessary to raise your voice."
She paused and looked down for a moment.
Then she looked at him. "Victor, how well do you
recall the things that took place Thursday when
Gary was taken? Pittsburgh? Do you really believe
that I could have known Thursday that anyone
could have taken or even planned to take Gary?"

"June, I planned to bring that up, but frankly,
you haven't taken the whole thing exactly as I

had expected. Seriously. I really expected you to be more understanding of my position. One thing has nothing to do with the other. You've got to realize that, on the one hand, I have no choice." He smiled for a moment as he glanced at her. "On the other hand, I see no reason why anything has to change between us. I don't want anything to change." He met and returned her intent stare, holding it and reinforcing it with his slight smile. "I hope you'll see it my way."

She continued to stare at him.

"I've given this considerable thought, June, and feel it's the only sensible way to handle this thing from all sides and for all concerned."

She continued to stare at him.

"And I'll see that you have a number, in fact, a selection, an abundance of other situations, good situations, from which to choose. Fred is already working on this." He continued to meet her studying eyes head on. To defect would be a sign of weakness. "This will be easy," he continued, "because I have so many friends who are so envious of me because of you." He hesitated for a moment and then smiled. "Because of your unquestioned excellence as an executive secretary."

She continued to sit quietly and look at him.

"I think it best that you don't take another job for a few weeks. But then, this has been a rather trying experience for all of us. To say the least. You could use a little time off, I'm sure. A little trip somewhere, perhaps. And whatever you do, don't worry about money. I'll handle that."

"Mr. Feldman," she said with a slight smile of

her own, "you're a remarkable man. Truly remarkable. Even after all these years here with you, I didn't really know just how remarkable you are." She stood up and started to leave.

"I hope you won't leave town for a day or two. I plan to be in touch with you before you go."

"Really?" She started toward the door, keeping her eyes on him.

"I would like to know where you'll be going on your little vacation trip."

"Really?"

"Perhaps I'll even see you there."

Her smile broadened. "Really?"

"Really," he said with his mock-warm smile.

"If you'll excuse me, Mr. Feldman, I have to go clean out my desk." She turned and walked out of the room, closing the door quietly.

He continued smiling until the door clicked. Then the smile quickly faded from his face.

34

Gary Feldman stayed in the hospital two days. He really wasn't very sick. He had been disappointed. He had been on his way to adventure, new experiences, distant places, California, San Francisco, Disneyland, mountains, great forests, the Pacific Ocean, who knows what else. He had been in the hands of a kidnapper who treated him like a pal. This was something to tell somebody about, if he had had somebody to tell. He had been in a getaway car. Yeah. A getaway car. Getting away. On the way. Pikes Peak. The Grand Canyon. A 747 flying coast to coast.

And then he'd been asked to get out of the getaway car. Get out of the car and walk into a greasy diner and tell them who he was. Who he was and that's all. Tell them nothing about Banner or the Pacific Ocean. There had been no reason to tell them anything else. Banner said so. There had been no reason not to do what Banner had told him not to do. And there had been good reason to do exactly what Banner had told him to do.

Banner had promised to come back for him. And the plan would only work if it were kept a secret. A perfect secret. An absolute secret.

Gary came home from the hospital with an impressive array of expensive medication. George Berman called at the house regularly at first and then less regularly as Gary showed the expected improvement from the rather severe respiratory complications stemming from his traumatic several days in the hands of his abductors. Isobel Feldman stayed close to her son, mothering, catering, doting, clucking, especially on the several occasions police and FBI personnel came to see him. She played games with him, watched television with him, listened to records with him, planned all her meals around eating with him. She gave up, during the two weeks or so following his arrival home from the hospital, all the things she normally did when she was not away on her travels. She did not go into the city. She did not go to the club. She did not shop. She did not leave the house or Gary. Her friends came to her, and she entertained them for lunch or in the afternoon, always with Gary close at hand.

She arranged a bridge gathering, at the suggestion of one of her friends, who had observed the way she was shutting herself in with him, especially since it was almost August, potentially Gary's worst season, and she insisted that Gary could stay right there with all the women. He wandered among the three tables, paying little attention to the twelve beams of concentrated maternal radiation being focused on him. After a few minutes, because he felt his mother wanted him to stay in the room, he got a volume of an illustrated encyclopedia and sat down to browse through it, creasing his little brows in concentration in spite of the cackling background of twelve-handed social bridge.

After nearly three weeks of self-imposed isolation from the world around her, Isobel was certain, quite certain, that she needed a rest and vacation. She even elicited a comment of support from George Berman that it was all right to leave now. After all, things had quieted down and returned to normal. Most important, Gary was his old self again. She was the one that needed therapy now. She needed desperately to get away, to unwind. She planned a few weeks away in the Caribbean, the Virgin Islands.

By the time Isobel left for the islands, the story of the kidnapping was completely out of the news. Roy Walls was in prison. Harry Banner was still at large, but since he had released the child and gotten away with only twenty-five thousand dollars, interest in his pursuit was hardly newsworthy after more than three weeks. The most intriguing detail of the entire case, as far as the authorities were concerned, was the fact that the child adamantly refused to discuss or even acknowledge any fact about Harry Banner, even that he had been seen with Banner by the policemen in the parking lot at the discount store. They had failed in several interrogations, first at the hospital and afterward at home, to get him to recount his experiences while held captive. Isobel adjudged this a hopefully harmless symptom of the shock his system had endured. Victor wrote it off as a vagary of his nonaverage child's mystique.

A few days after Isobel had left on her trip to the Caribbean, Gary received a phone call. This fact went unnoticed because of his practice of answering the phone and taking all calls and messages during the day. By the time he was seven years old he had developed this practice. It gave him something to do, and Victor Feldman supported him because he got the messages correct and complete, at least to a greater extent than Sara had ever been able to do. As a result, when the phone rang during the day, Gary usually ran to answer it, and Sara generally ignored it unless it rang at some length.

After Gary received the call, his entire demeanor changed. He became gay, excited, almost giddy. No one noticed the abruptness of the change, only that a pleasant change had taken or was in the process of taking place. At last he was really coming out of it, shrugging off any last vestigial effects of his experience.

On the Thursday following his secret phone call Gary's giddiness became nervous exhilaration. He paced around the large house, constantly checking clocks, pushing himself from books to television to the piano, unable to become absorbed in any of them. He slid his lunch around on the plate, finally leaving most of it.

At five minutes to three in the afternoon he walked into the foyer and stood motionless, listening to the sounds of the house. Sara was in the kitchen with her radio. He could not hear Jane-eta upstairs. He went into the library and over to the gerbil tank. He reached in, lifted out the two tiny brownish animals and gently placed one in each pants pocket. Then he tiptoed to the front door and unhooked the recently installed chain latch, easing it down to a silent hanging posture. Up on tiptoes, he turned the recently installed deadlatch with his left hand, the doorknob with his right. He pulled the door open soundlessly and looked out.

He looked back into the house for a moment and then stepped out, closing the door quietly. He strode down the long driveway, turned right at the street, walked to the dead-end intersection and turned right again. Passing an area of wild brush between lawns, he stopped, took the gerbils out of his pockets, squatted and placed them on the ground in the brush. He watched as they darted away, stopping here and there to stand up on their haunches and look about them. He walked several hundred yards to a small side road and turned right again, coming to a large shiny parked car. The man driving had black-brown hair, a short but full-face beard, brown flecked with gray, and a very elegant, dark blue tropical suit and tie. He looked at the man, first expectantly and then in confusion. On seeing the man smile, he broke into a happy grin. "Hey, Banner, I didn't recognize you." He hurriedly climbed into the car and dropped himself onto the front seat next to Harry. "Are we going to California now, Banner?"

Harry grabbed the boy by his small shoulder

and gave him a good-natured, twisting shove toward the back seat. "Get back there and get under that blanket until we get out of here."

The child scrambled over and disappeared under a cotton quilt on the floor of the car. "Are we going to California now?" His voice was muffled by the quilt.

"Did you leave the note like I told you?"

"Yes. Are we going to California now?"

"First we take you and dye that red hair."

"Then are we going to California?"

"Probably."

"Are we going to call my father from California?"

"We'll have to call him from somewhere. He still owes me quite a bit of money." Then, as an afterthought, almost an aside: "And he's getting a— Why, Christ, it's the best money he ever spent."

"What?"

"Nothing, Redhead. Relax."

But the boy had heard him. He just did not quite understand what Banner had meant. More ransom? But what difference did it make? Who cared? He shrugged his shoulders and swept it out of his mind, preferring to think instead of points west, mountains and oceans, things to see and do. . . .

*If you enjoy the macabre,
the unexpected . . .
here are gems of death
and horror from the
world's most unfettered
imaginations.*

ALFRED
HITCHCOCK
presents:

ALFRED HITCHCOCK'S DEATH BAG 75c
COFFIN CORNER 75c
GAMES KILLERS PLAY 75c
GET ME TO THE WAKE ON TIME 75c
HANGMAN'S DOZEN 60c
HAPPINESS IS A WARM CORPSE 75c
A HARD DAY AT THE SCAFFOLD 75c
MORE STORIES FOR LATE AT NIGHT 75c
MORE STORIES NOT FOR THE NERVOUS 75c
MURDERS I FELL IN LOVE WITH 75c
MURDERS ON THE HALF SKULL 75c
NOOSE REPORT 75c
SCREAM ALONG WITH ME 75c
SKULL SESSION 75c
STORIES NOT FOR THE NERVOUS 75c
TWELVE STORIES FOR LATE AT NIGHT 75c
SLAY RIDE 75c

DELL BOOKS

DELIVERANCE

by James Dickey

This novel, by one of America's finest poets, is a tale of violent adventure and inner discovery. Four men embark on a canoe trip down a wild section of a river in the heartland of today's South. When two of the group are attacked viciously and perversely by mountaineers, a mildly adventurous canoe trip explodes into a gruesome nightmare of horror and murder.

If you cannot obtain copies of this title from your local bookseller, just send the price (plus 15c per copy for handling and postage) to Dell Books, Post Office Box 1000, Pinebrook, N. J. 07058. No postage or handling charge is required on any order of five or more books.

How many of these Dell bestsellers have you read?

THE SENSUOUS WOMAN by "J" $1.25

DELIVERANCE by James Dickey $1.25

BALL FOUR by Jim Bouton $1.25

THE ANDERSON TAPES by Lawrence Sanders $1.25

MARY QUEEN OF SCOTS by Antonia Fraser $1.50

THE AMERICAN HERITAGE DICTIONARY 75c

MILE HIGH by Richard Condon $1.25

THE VALUE OF NOTHING by John Weitz $1.25

THE ESTATE by Isaac Bashevis Singer $1.25

PATTON by Ladislas Farago $1.25

THE ANDROMEDA STRAIN by Michael Crichton $1.25

THE POSEIDON ADVENTURE by Paul Gallico $1.25

THE DOCTOR'S QUICK WEIGHT LOSS DIET by Irwin M. Stillman, M. D. and Samm Sinclair Baker 95c

SOUL ON ICE by Eldridge Cleaver 95c

THE $20,000,000 HONEYMOON by Fred Sparks 95c

If you cannot obtain copies of these titles from your local bookseller, just send the price (plus 15c per copy for handling and postage) to Dell Books, Post Office Box 1000, Pinebrook, N. J. 07058. No postage or handling charge is required on any order of five or more books.